K

Part 1: Destin

Chapters 1 – 15

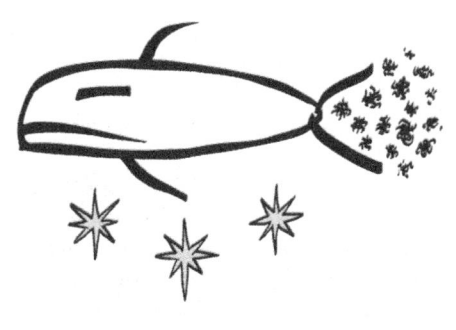

To Jim,
Wishing you and yours long life,
health, and happiness!

By Leslee Sheu

Leslee
Sheu

Kumasagi, Part 1: Destin
(Chapters 1 – 15)

Copyright © 2020 Leslee Sheu

Edited by Claire Levine.
Cover illustration by Joshua Esmeralda.
Interior illustrations by Leslee Sheu.
Special thanks to Elissa Saunders.

www.LesleeSheu.com

ISBN: 979-8-66762-735-7

CONTENTS

~ PROLOGUE ~

Years of frustration had transformed Najat into a brooding, cold man. In public, it was rare to witness even a squint of emotion on his face. In private, if he was alone, he sometimes let slip a squint or two.

The love of his life was in childbirth, and the child was not his.

Najat stayed away, retreating into the solitude of his quarters. He sweated and paced, as any father would. He grimaced and cursed, as a father would not. He was not concerned with the child, of course. His hands burned red from wringing out his concern for *her*. A second pregnancy was dangerous, for any woman—Najat's own mother had died because she bore a second child.

Najat came to a wall and stopped pacing. He could have Felt Asta from where he stood, if he didn't respect her wish for some physical and mental distance between them. He didn't respect that wish, actually, but he respected her. He loved her. Najat rested his forehead against the wall as terror roared across his nerves. He had secretly observed her two days before, and her pale, wan appearance had frightened him.

Najat moved to a window facing the direction of Asta, and peered out into nothing. The temple complex lay dark and quiet under the poor light of the stars. He continued to stand there until he became agitated beyond the point of obedience. He was perfectly within his rights to monitor her wellbeing.

Suddenly resolute, Najat seated himself in preparation to reach out to her. He straightened his spine . . . calmed his breathing . . . cleared his thoughts . . . and then immediately sensed someone approach the entrance to his quarters.

He stood up again, listening. Seconds later, the bell chimed at the door, augmented by a hesitant knock.

Najat had sent his attendants away, so there was no one to answer for him. He stumbled slightly as he walked through the front room, and his fingers slipped at the locks. He knew who stood on the other side. For the second time in his life, Najat opened his door to the midwife's son.

While the boy stood doubled over, catching his breath, Najat had time to slip on a mask of outward composure. Had she died? No, he would have Felt it, he was sure. But why would the midwife's son rush all this way to tell him that the child had been born? Najat found himself flushed with annoyance.

"Mathin!" Najat said in his great booming voice, causing the boy to snap to attention, chest still heaving.

"Mahasagi," Mathin gasped, flashing his hands in a quick mudra of respect. "Come with me!"

Incomprehension prevented Najat from moving. "To . . .

the birthing house?"

"Yes, please hurry!"

"Your ama—"

"No, it's Gampo-Saati! She's asking for you. Ama said it's alright!"

Asta! Najat lost his focus on the boy's face. He did not expect a summons from her, even with all of the reasons—some hoped for and some dreaded—that she might. And why did she ask for him via Mathin when she could have just—

"Saat, please!" Mathin regained Najat's attention. "You should hurry. She isn't well."

Such news caused all caution to evaporate. Of course she wasn't well! Najat leapt past the boy, sprinted across the foyer, and thudded down the switchback stairs before he remembered that a hint of composure might be necessary.

He didn't know Mathin was following close behind, and the boy had to pull several maneuvers to avoid running into Najat's backside as the man halted at the bottom of the stairs. Mathin skirted past him and led the way outside, pointing down the lamplit lane in the direction he had come. "Past Medical Arts, turn right—it's the annex across the lane. Someone will be waiting!"

Najat already knew the location. He stripped off his robes and threw them to the boy, then ran in a dignified manner toward the lane in his loincloth. The lane was a slim canal that connected most parts of the temple complex. Flat stones paved each side of the water for those who preferred to walk. For the Mahasagi, swimming was faster. Without slowing down at the edge, Najat executed a neat side dive into the lane and took off with smooth, powerful strokes toward the Medical Arts building.

The night-cooled water did not provide comfort. Najat berated himself for staying so far from her. It was a fair distance to the Medical Arts building—the boy could run faster than swim, but still, it must have taken precious time to reach Najat's quarters. Najat kicked harder, trying to redeem time, trying to redeem everything. His webbed hands sheared huge arcs through the water. He cut under one footbridge, then a second, as the north face of the temple loomed by on his left, too slowly. Then—finally— the greenery that fringed the walls of the Medical Arts building began flashing by on his right. Another footbridge. The Mahasagi was known for his remarkable aquatic speed, but tonight it felt like he was crawling through sand.

Lamplight illuminated an intersection in the lane. Najat struggled to clear his mind as he took the right turn with a smooth sidestroke. An archway rose up ahead of him, part of an elevated walk that connected the Medical Arts building to its satellites. In the expanded lamplight under the arch, an attendant leaned out over the water, watching for him. Najat slowed his stroke to convey an appearance of calm. No one knew of his feelings for Asta. Any displays of emotion must be kept in the acceptable realm of a man's concern for his brother's wife.

The attendant—one of Maore's—stepped back as Najat pulled himself out of the water. "Mahasagi," she said, as his shadow fell across her face. Her mudra was hampered by the clean robes she held in her arms. The towering figure and stern demeanor of Najat Gampoban had the unintended effect of intimidating those who saw him for the first time. Even standing there in his loincloth, shaking

4

excess water from his long limbs, he exuded a certain dignity unsurpassed by other men.

Without waiting for directions from the attendant, Najat opened his mind and located Asta within the walls of the building. The attendant found herself trotting after him as he headed for the nearest entrance.

"Oh! Saat . . . !" She had to tug at his arm to get his attention. Najat grunted at the reminder, taking the robes from her and pulling them on as he continued into the building. It would not do for the Mahasagi to arrive in Maore's domain wearing only his underwear.

Using Asta's waning energy as a beacon, he chose the correct corridor and hastened to the room he Felt she was in. Maore herself met him at the door. The midwife bowed and lifted her hands in the mudra of respect as he entered the damp chamber. Each of the attendants in the room briefly stopped her work to face him and echo the midwife's gesture.

"Come." Maore gestured for him to follow her around the edge of the circular birthing pool. The strange pink tint of the water caught Najat's attention, and as they neared the opposite side he saw a wet trail leading from the tiled edge of the pool, a trail that graduated from diluted pink to viscous red as it met the foot of the low couch where Asta lay.

They had to step over the trail to reach Asta's side. Two women who had been hovering over the bed moved back as Najat approached. Even Maore remained a few feet behind as he knelt at Asta's shoulder.

Asta's eyes met his with unexpected clarity. Najat recognized the brightness in those eyes and his heart jumped—Asta was dying. Every muscle and nerve in his body strained to keep his face relaxed and his demeanor calm. He wanted to scream at the sight of her. Her hardening, cracked skin, the fluid at her nose and mouth, her paralyzed limbs—many others had died beneath his hand, yet he could not bear watching it happen to *her*. He permitted himself a gentle touch at her brow, but then his hand trembled so tellingly that he had to withdraw it.

Najat broke contact with those shining gray eyes and abruptly stood, disregarding a meek sound of protest from Asta. He turned to look at Maore. The plump, usually cheerful midwife shook her head, moving in to adjust the blanket that covered Asta's lower half. "We tried . . ." she said, indicating a dark patch of blood that saturated most of the fabric. The patch was still spreading.

Hearing Najat's intake of breath, Maore cut him off, "We *tried*. We sent for a doctor, but she put him to sleep before he could get here. She won't let anyone help. She won't even let Amala Tebbe come." Maore lowered her voice. "Talk to her. She asked for *you*. I think . . . she wants you to . . ."

"Mm," Najat rumbled, to indicate he understood. Yet— had Asta really given up? Why wouldn't she accept those who might save her? *He* couldn't save her—he could only guide her, at the time death.

She was certainly dying. He could Feel *that* excruciatingly well from where he stood. Instinct took over, all feelings shoved aside. In front of Maore, Najat must behave as if he had no other reason to be here.

He knelt beside Asta again. This time, her searching eyes did not meet his directly. He knew he couldn't talk to her as the midwife had suggested, because Asta's senses were now dissolving one by one. She could no longer hear him. Her sight was failing, and she could not taste or smell. By this time her body would be numb, unable to feel his reassuring touch at her arm.

As the Mahasagi, Najat was intimately familiar with each stage of the dying process. He prepared to do for Asta what he had done for so many others. He would assist her consciousness as it transferred from her body, to make sure she was in a state of peace. The Mahasagi was there to purify the mind and spirit as the body died.

Najat Gampoban was a disciplined master of his craft, no matter that he had become a troubled soul. He was capable of shielding his own dark corners from the increased clairvoyance of the dying. Only those who had passed on knew of the warm, clear light that resided at the very core of the Mahasagi's being.

Now, with eyes and knees on the wet tiles, Najat tucked his own pain away and put his heart into summoning that light for his beloved Asta.

As Najat gingerly opened a line to her, preparing to merge his awareness with hers, he sensed that this was not the only reason she had summoned him to her deathbed. Her bloodless lips could no longer speak, but she had something to tell him. He Felt her waiting for him.

A sudden, intuitive urge caused him to hesitate. "Wait," he whispered, even as he felt himself sliding into a trance that was not his own. Asta's process of dying had accelerated, and it was pulling him in.

Maore stood a few paces from the bed, skeptically checking Najat's technique. His posture towards Asta had such a tenderness to it that Maore chided herself—after all, Najat Gampoban had done this countless times. Deciding that he must have things under control, the midwife finally stepped back to let the Mahasagi do his work.

A flash of color caught the corner of Maore's eye. She turned to see her son standing in the doorway, with the wadded mass of Najat's traditional blue robes slung over one shoulder. The boy watched the scene across the birthing pool, mesmerized. As a mother determined to shield her child from the reality of death, Maore leapt around the pool to plant her girth between Mathin and his view of the room.

"Thank you, dear, thank you." She patted his flushed cheek and took the clothes he carried for Najat. Mathin tried to sneak another peek around his mother's wide hip, but she flicked open the robes, deftly blocking her son's view as she shook wrinkles from the heavy fabric. She used the wide cloth to shepherd Mathin into the corridor. "Now, it's getting late—"

"But how is she?" Mathin looked up at Maore. His beautifully concerned eyes put a lump in the midwife's throat. The boy had planted himself directly outside the door from the moment he found out that his cherished auntie was in labor. It was too difficult to tell him the truth.

"We won't really know until the morning," she lied. "It's a good thing you brought the Mahasagi. He can help her." Maore had sent the boy on the errand just to give him something meaningful to do. Now she propelled him away from the birthing room with a stern hand on his shoulder. "Go back to the house. Get some sleep, kuma-la."

Mathin yawned hugely at the suggestion. Yet he could

not leave things so easily. "What about her baby? Is he going to be okay?" Mathin had wanted to see the baby, at least.

His mother turned back to the birthing room. "Get some sleep," she repeated. "I'll see you in the morning." To prevent further argument, she closed the door behind her.

Her son's question was a reminder—there was a baby to tend to. After carefully hanging Najat's clothes on a wall hook near the door, Maore stole around the opposite side of the pool, glancing at the couch on her way. The brittle form of Asta lay immobile on the wet cushions as the lithe form of the Mahasagi knelt unmoving beside her. Creased effort on Asta's face represented a struggle. No woman could go peacefully knowing she must leave behind a newborn.

Maore's eldest attendant waited in a far corner of the humid room, holding the cleaned and swaddled baby. The midwife approached, swallowing hard against the tragic scene. The attendant was weeping.

"Shush, shush," Maore chided the woman, taking the child from her. The baby was content, with open, calm eyes. Swaddled as he was, he looked healthy and well-formed. Each tiny hand displayed five tiny webbed fingers, all properly developed. He was a good weight and length. His facial features were as well-proportioned as an infant's features could be. Maore marveled as the child cooed at her.

Maore's attendant wiped the tears away and put on a more professional face. Maore was gratified. They had to plan what to do with the child, and she needed her women to have their wits about them. She was about to give instructions to her attendant when the woman suddenly jumped and let out a teeny gasp, staring past Maore's shoulder. The midwife turned around to see what had startled her attendant, and almost dropped the child.

Najat Gampoban stood behind them.

The midwife reflexively clutched the baby more securely to her chest. There was a strange look in Najat's brown eyes as he stared toward some vague area between Maore's face and the bundle in her arms. She wasn't sure if she should speak to him—he seemed to still be in a trance. He took a step closer, prompting her to blurt out, "Mahasagi?"

Najat finally spoke. "The child . . ."

"Mahasagi?" the midwife repeated, trying to gain his attention. Why had he left Asta's side? Had Gampo-Saati passed on? Najat continued to walk toward the confused Maore. Candlelight caught a sheen of perspiration across the dark bronze dome of his shaved head.

Suddenly Najat's eyes snapped to catch Maore's. "Asta must see the child. She must see the child before she goes." He spoke clearly, his deep voice commanding. Apparently Asta was still alive.

"But—the baby is . . . is . . ." There was a reason Maore had not already shown the child to his mother. "Look," she told Najat, lifting the cloth that covered the newborn's lower half. She cocked her arm to show the Mahasagi what she had trouble articulating.

One massive hand closed firmly around the midwife's upper arm. Najat pulled her forward to get a closer look at the child. Normally fearless, Maore gulped as the towering Mahasagi's breath fanned her forehead. Her nearest attendant scurried backwards into the shadows. Najat ignored their reactions to his peculiar behavior as he inspected the naked child. The baby's dark legs, so similar in color to Najat's own skin, kicked in healthy reaction to the sudden draft where Maore held the cloth away.

"Mm," Najat grunted, and his grip on Maore's arm tightened. His face darkened as the reason for her concern became clear. Finally he released her arm and straightened his spine, holding her eyes with his. "She must see him, regardless. Cover that part."

Najat stepped aside and motioned for Maore to precede him toward the couch where Asta lay. His iron stare crushed any chance of rebellion. Tucking the swaddling cloth securely around the baby's legs and abdomen, the midwife obeyed.

The blanched form of Asta appeared as a corpse. Her stiff hands lay red on the blood-soaked blanket. Her cold arms lay white against the dark, wet cushions. Asta's eyes were open to the ceiling, but Maore knew that the woman could not see. The young mother was already dead.

"No," Najat rumbled, "She is still here." He clutched Maore's bruised arm again, dragging her the last few steps to Asta. The midwife's bolder attendants flinched at Najat's rough handling of their mistress. Maore saw their protective stance and shook her head at them, willing them to step back. The young women submitted, but their watchful eyes remained to comfort her.

Prodded by the Mahasagi, the midwife leaned toward Asta's body. It was awkward, trying to show the child to an unresponsive, prone figure. Maore tilted the bundle as well as she could without spilling the baby onto his mother's frigid chest.

11

"Here." Najat's voice sounded impatient in her ear. He touched Maore's arm again, but this time a gentle warmth spread from his fingers. Alarmed, the midwife felt the muscles across her shoulders and chest relax. Her arms went limp under the weight of the child.

The Mahasagi reached in and pulled the bundle from Maore's weakened grip. "Stay back!" he said to Maore's angry attendants. The midwife watched helplessly as Najat knelt beside Asta again, placing soft fingers on the seemingly deceased woman's brow. His other long arm cradled the whimpering baby, who began to fuss and kick.

"Shhh!" he shot at the women around him. No one moved. Bowing his head, he slid back into his silent dialogue with Asta. After a few moments, even the newborn fell quiet. Maore's strength returned, but she felt a strange fog settling in her head. She stepped closer to the couch, trying to understand what was happening.

Suddenly, amazingly, Asta's body moved. One hand slid in the blood at her hip as her shoulders began to tremble. Her saliva-encrusted mouth cracked open. Asta let out a loud and raspy moan, freezing the hearts of the women surrounding her.

Najat pulled away and stood up, towering over the women again. "Assist her! She wants to sit up!"

Incredulous, the women hesitated. Finally, Maore herself hurried forward when Asta's whole body began to convulse. The Mahasagi stepped back and enveloped the newborn securely with both arms as Maore's attendants muscled past him to help their mistress.

Asta's eyes came alive again, rolling madly as she raggedly gasped for air. The women struggled to get their arms under her slippery, heaving shoulders.

"Support her head!" Maore directed them. Slowly they lifted Asta's dripping torso from the soggy couch. "Cover her back!" Asta was halfway sitting now, trembling at the verge of consciousness as the women supported her back with strong arms and dry blankets. Maore struggled to hold down Asta's twitching arms. It would still be difficult to show her the baby this way.

Asta's head lolled forward. Maore lifted one arm to shove Asta's head back up by the chin and hold it in place. "Asta . . . Asta!" Maore tried to get her attention. Beneath clinging strands of white, wet hair, Asta's eyelids fluttered. Finally, with a certain amount of steadiness, her eyes fell open on Maore.

"Mahasagi," Maore summoned Najat to bring the baby. She kept her eyes on Asta's face, willing the woman to stay focused. Asta's lips quivered blue against Maore's thumb. She was trying to speak.

"Suuu . . ." Her breath fell on Maore with a heavy smell. The women all leaned in, trying to grasp her words.

Asta had nothing to say. Her eyes rolled back. She convulsed again, a test of muscle power for the women supporting her.

"Mahasagi!" said Maore, as Asta stopped moving and sagged in the women's straining arms. Najat did not step forward. Maore looked up and saw only her dazed attendants. The candle-dim chamber beyond was empty.

Najat Gampoban had vanished, along with Asta's newborn child.

~ CHAPTER 1 ~

It was Najat's brother, Jayan, who triggered the events that would bring Najat and Asta together. It happened before Najat became the Mahasagi, yet well after the brothers had settled into adulthood. People had started to whisper about Jayan, who at the late age of thirty still hadn't bought a wife.

Jayan Gampoban was a restless fellow, an explorer who would disappear into the wilderness for years at a time. He had no home of his own, so when he felt the need to recuperate between adventures, he would stay with his father on Sindhupat Island or drop into Shakti Lake City to see Najat.

During his second expedition into the mountains that lay west of Shakti-Patal Plateau, Jayan contracted a strange virus. He didn't fall ill from it himself—his immune system was tough after meeting numerous exotic pathogens in other parts of the world. He arrived in Shakti Lake City exhausted and hungry and pungently unwashed, but beneath all that he seemed healthy.

As usual, he didn't send word to his brother that he was coming. He found Najat's empty dorm apartment and fell into Najat's simple bed. Najat discovered him there that evening, splay-limbed and snoring.

Jayan remained that way until dawn, when the morning chimes woke him and all the divers housed in the dormitory. His bleary eyes eventually focused on Najat, who sat in a meditative pose among tussled bedding on the floor, gazing toward the wall. Hearing his older brother stir, Najat cut his eyes toward Jayan and scowled fondly. They had not seen each other in almost two years.

They skipped any exchange of sentimental greetings. Najat knew Jayan's routine: sleep through the first day, eat through the second. The dorm cook prepared a lavish breakfast and delivered it straight to Najat's apartment himself, trailing several excited divers behind him. The young diving trainees jostled to catch a glimpse of the great Jayan Gampoban, while the older divers who knew Jayan hovered nearby, simply hoping to greet him.

Najat shooed them all away and closed his door, only opening it again for those who delivered lunch and dinner. The brothers communed privately for the rest of the day, feeding themselves on the cook's finest offerings and feeding each other on two years' worth of stories.

Late that night, when the dormitory was dark and all the other residents asleep, Najat led Jayan out to the bathhouse for a much-needed scrubbing. Then Najat took back his own bed after making sure that Jayan was comfortable on an extra mat. They kept talking, enjoying their last few undisturbed moments together before finally falling asleep. By the time they woke the next morning, word had spread through the city that Jayan Gampoban was in for a visit.

That was Jayan's third day, the busy day. This time the door was open at breakfast, and scores of messengers bowed their way through it bearing appointment requests for Jayan.

He groaned and whispered to Najat, "The academics descend!" Scientific scholars from the city's two universities were eager to see the journals and specimens from his latest travels. Jayan's groans were in jest—he always enjoyed this part of a visit. He accepted each invitation, even if it did make for a hectic schedule over the next few days.

Najat told the disappointed divers, "He's staying with me, so you'll see plenty of him. He'll show up at meal times, most likely!"

The next morning, Jayan appeared at the Udaka Ruby to watch the divers swim.

The Udaka Ruby was the centerpiece of the diver complex. It was the divers' famed training venue, an immense rectangular pool of red-hued water accentuated at two corners with jutting boulders. The multi-leveled dormitory surrounded it, so that all rooms faced in toward the pool.

Anyone could see the Ruby from the balcony walkways and open-air staircases that connected the complex, but the best place to watch training was from the stone theater seating along the great length of the pool. Jayan sat two rows up toward the middle, along with a fluctuating number of younger divers who came to ogle at him when they weren't needed in the water.

Thinly veiled curiosity bubbled under the divers' polite conversation. Their eyes searched Jayan's features, then flicked to the water where Najat swam. Jayan knew they were looking for a resemblance. Each of the two Gampobans was famous in his own right, but together they presented an additional novelty, by the very fact that they were brothers. Even Jayan, in all his travels, had never encountered a family with more than one child.

The divers were not disappointed—Jayan and Najat looked very much alike.

Jayan's hands were another point of interest for the divers, who all had fully webbed fingers like Najat. The tough adventurer loved the land more than water, but the land was rough on the hands he had been born with. So he had chosen to have the webbing surgically removed, a common practice for farmers, craftsmen, and laborers.

Jayan was showing the divers the faint scars between his fingers when they all heard a yell from the direction of the pool.

"Ai! Najat's losing!"

Everyone's attention snapped to the water. Najat—the oldest, strongest, and fastest of the divers—was being matched stroke for stroke by one of the junior divers in a heated race. The divers standing at the pool's edge bellowed at the two in the water, incoherent in their excitement.

"But . . . he's not losing," Jayan said to the diver next to him, "They're about even."

"Gavind is ahead!" shouted someone behind them.

"No! Najat's still in front!" yelled another.

The diver next to Jayan told him, "No one has ever been

this close. I wouldn't even try, myself. But Gavind always tries—"

The rest of the young men around Jayan bounded from their seats and rushed to the edge of the pool. The diver next to him remained, providing commentary. "One more lap after this one. Najat is just playing. There's no way he'll let Gavind win, not with you here . . . and the Mahasagi watching, too . . ."

Jayan looked to see the Mahasagi standing at one end of the pool, flanked by two attendants. The man was very old, but he stood solidly enough, silent and still in his blue robes. His silver eyes watched the two divers in the water. Jayan looked back at the water to see Najat and Gavind Sandarapan make the turn at the end of the pool opposite the Mahasagi, flipping in unison.

The water of the Udaka Ruby was indeed ruby-like in color because it came through a channel from Shakti Lake. The divers did their work in that lake, so it was important that their training venue use the same water, full of the same minerals. Under the strong, late-morning sunlight, those minerals caused a fascinating play of color in the water. Jayan thought it looked like the cranberry juice he had sipped at breakfast. As they pushed off from the far wall, Gavind and Najat could only be seen as two purple shadows beneath the water.

The other divers leaned dangerously over the edge, suddenly quiet. When the two racers broke the surface a quarter of the way back toward the Mahasagi, the spectators exploded into deafening whoops and bellows. Gavind was still beside Najat, but his stroke appeared erratic next to Najat's swift, solid arcs. The divers screamed Gavind's nickname, "*Sandi! Sandi!*"

Gavind could hear them from the water, but their words were unintelligible through the roaring of his own blood in his ears. He could not mask the tremendous effort it took to keep up with Najat. His aching lungs and shaking muscles showed themselves as the water splashed too high around him. Najat swam on his air side, so with each gasping breath Gavind could see the older diver still next to him.

The two men had bonded from the day Gavind attained junior status two years earlier—Najat as gruff teacher, Gavind as awe-struck student. As Gavind fought now in the red water, he assumed that Najat must be letting him get this close in order to challenge him. The junior diver put on a final burst of speed, determined to not disappoint his cheering comrades or the beloved mentor beside him.

Najat's own mentor, the current Mahasagi, stood waiting as the pair flew the remaining length to his end of the pool. Jayan watched silently from his seat. The first hand to hit the wall was Najat's, sloshing water a few inches over the edge. Najat lifted his head from the water but did not look up. Gavind arrived with a great splash, fully drenching both feet of one of the Mahasagi's attendants. A terrific cheer went up from the other divers, who admired Gavind's efforts even if he hadn't won.

Ram, the senior diver in charge of that morning's training, crouched down at the edge of the pool near Gavind. "Sandarapan, don't give up!" he said to the panting, trembling diver, "You'll beat him yet!"

Gavind couldn't tell if Ram meant this as genuine encouragement or a joke—surely everyone realized that Najat had been toying with him. "Thanks," he gasped, still struggling to catch his breath.

Ram stood up and shouted to the others, "That's all for now! Visibility drills after lunch!" After some hurried but respectful bows in the direction of the Mahasagi, the divers scattered to get cleaned up for lunch. Ram found Jayan and invited him to join them for the meal. The Mahasagi conferred quietly with his attendants, preparing to return to the temple buildings located on the south side of the lake.

Still in the water, Gavind turned to Najat. At first he didn't notice how Najat clung to the tiled lip of the pool. Najat was quick to pull one arm free and clasp hands with Gavind, smiling at the younger diver's sheepish manner.

"Ah . . ." Gavind started. He wanted to tell Najat that he would try even harder the next time, but he didn't want to sound too eager to beat his friend—but surely Najat was trying to toughen him, so a competitive manner might be expected—

"Good race," said Najat, giving Gavind's hand a hearty squeeze.

Gavind stared at the older diver. The handshake might have been hearty, but the voice was not. Najat's words came out in a raspy whisper, bearing no resemblance to his usual deep, clear vocal resonance. Although Najat's voice did not yet have the mystical rumble it would be known for in later years, he could still be identified by his commanding bass tone. This faltering whisper surprised Gavind. Something was wrong.

Then it got worse—Najat wheezed audibly on his next intake of breath. His hand splashed free from Gavind's and he clung to the wall again, staring down at the water. He wheezed softly, slowly, concentrating hard to keep his breath steady.

"Kumasagi!" Gavind said. The junior diver looked around for help. Ram and Jayan walked toward the building, deep in conversation. The Mahasagi pointed toward the lake and said something to his nodding attendants. The other divers were heading for their dorm rooms to get ready for lunch.

"Najat, are you alright?" Gavind moved closer to his friend, but the older diver raised a hand to stop him. Najat scowled down at the water, clearing his throat. He did not look at Gavind. With a sudden movement he thrust his arms over the edge and pulled himself out of the pool.

The younger diver remained floating in puzzlement as Najat walked away from him, in the opposite direction from the Mahasagi. The wizened old man turned his head slightly and watched his twin soul from the corner of an eye. But the future Mahasagi moved quickly to disappear up the nearest staircase, keeping his shoulders squared and strong as if nothing had happened.

~ CHAPTER 2 ~

Jayan and the divers dug into lunch without waiting for Najat, who went missing after the race with Gavind. They ate in a small hall with big windows, a gathering room reserved for the junior and senior divers. Younger boys lived and studied at the complex, but only those who had achieved junior status could train, work, and eat with the seniors.

Eight men, including Jayan, sat around the low table. The divers, slim but well cut, with cleanly shaved heads like Najat, sat tall on their cushions in folded leg poses. Jayan, burly and wide, with the same bronze skin as Najat, sat hunched over the table, almost off his cushion in an effort to reach all of the excellent food. He had spicy sauce stuck up to his knuckles from smashing lentils and rice together with his fingers. He shoveled it all into his mouth with a rhythmic canter that didn't slow even when he chose to speak.

The divers overlooked Jayan's coarse manners—they

admired his vigor. They also ate with their hands, if not as swiftly. Their collective poise at the table proved their true nature—these men endured rigorous mental training along with their swimming drills. They may have been rowdy at poolside during Gavind's race, but Jayan knew that each diver possessed an amazing level of inner control, which could be called on when needed. This skill was essential to their work.

Everyone was laughing now, showing few skills other than eating and throwing barbs in Gavind Sandarapan's direction. Gavind said little in return, maintaining a mouth full of food. His own uneasiness rested beneath a quick, false smile—no one else knew of Najat's earlier troubles. For the moment Gavind kept his thoughts to himself, wishing his lunch companions would find a subject for discussion other than the race.

"So what's all the rumpus about?" Jayan asked. "Don't you race each other all the time?"

"Sure, we race *each other*," said one of the junior divers, "but we don't race *him*." Jayan was still trying to remember names—that diver had introduced himself earlier as Palen.

"Najat is in some of the races," Ram said to Jayan. "He just gets so far ahead of everyone . . . we all end up battling for second place. It's like he's not even there."

"Sandarapan knows he's there!" said another diver from further down the table.

Everyone looked at Gavind. He bit into a spinach dumpling and chewed vigorously, keeping his eyes on the fascinating contents of his plate.

"*That's* what all the rumpus is about," said Palen, cocking a thumb toward Gavind, "He's the only one who will go against Najat with no one else in the Ruby."

The comment elicited a grunt from Gavind, his first contribution to the conversation.

"Where is Najat?" Ram asked. "Did anyone see him after . . . ?"

The other divers all looked at Jayan. He set down his empty plate and shook his head, mouth still full—he had been with Ram since leaving the Udaka Ruby.

They all turned to Gavind, but he shrugged and averted his eyes. Najat's wheezing attack worried him. Gavind had never seen or heard of Najat doing it before.

Ram prodded the junior diver. "Well, did he say anything before you left him?"

Gavind cringed under Ram's unfortunate choice of words. He should never have let Najat walk away. He wished he could tell the other divers his suspicions about Najat's health so that they might stop their ridiculous talking and go find him. But to suggest a moment of weakness in the future Mahasagi, especially in front of these men, would be unpardonable. Najat would never forgive him.

He said it anyway, not realizing his thoughts were escaping off his tongue until it was too late. "I think Najat isn't feeling w-well."

Seven pairs of eyebrows shot up in astonishment. Ram had just sipped some tea and almost choked on it. He swallowed quickly, clearing his mouth to say, "Do you mean, he's *ill?*"

"I'm . . . not sure . . ." Gavind hesitated, his loyalty to Najat kicking in somewhat belatedly. Everyone leaned toward him, expecting him to elaborate. Jayan looked concerned, but the divers' expressions revealed a mix of curiosity and skepticism. They only knew Najat as a specimen of invulnerability.

That specimen of invulnerability now stood in the stairwell below the lunching divers, leaning heavily against the handrail. Najat overheard Gavind's blunder on his way up to finally join the others, but that wasn't the only thing to make him pause. His lungs were cramping and he needed a rest to master his breath.

Najat listened to Gavind's voice as the junior diver attempted a dodge. "Then again, the Mahasagi spoke with him after he got out of the Ruby, so maybe that's why he's not here. Maybe he's eating with him . . ." Najat grimaced. Gavind's clumsy lie would not get past Ram. Gavind seemed to know that because he tumbled on, "So why was the Mahasagi here today, anyway?"

To Najat's relief, the sounds of eating started again. Ram answered, "He just said he wanted to watch us train. He doesn't need a specific reason."

Najat listened a bit more as the conversation went on. The pain in his chest had left for the moment, but he felt very tired, almost too tired to continue up the stairs. Then he heard his brother's concerned voice, "You're sure Najat is all right? You said before that he wasn't feeling well . . ."

Shut up, Jay! Najat thought, suddenly possessing ample energy for galloping up the remaining distance to the dining room.

He strode into the hall so pointedly that everyone saw him at once. Plates and cups clinked to the table, and backs straightened. No one spoke as Najat approached. Gavind studied his uneaten spinach dumplings while everyone else studied Najat, trying to sense his mood. Jayan and Ram scrambled apart to make room for him to sit. With a neutral expression on his face, Najat folded himself onto the cushion between them.

The divers all faced him and brought their palms together at chest level. "Kumasagi," Ram intoned, greeting Najat by his formal title.

Najat let the moment continue for another beat, then presented them all with a disarming, sheepish smile. It was counterfeit, but it worked. Relieved chuckles drifted from most quarters of the table. Najat shrugged and ducked his head like a boy as the divers started joking again about the race, throwing barbs at him now. They took his plate and heaped it with greens and dumplings and rice and lentils with spicy sauce, none of which he felt like eating.

The question of Najat's health had been forgotten— even Jayan did not pursue it. The others went back to the topic of the race. Ever the curious observer, Jayan asked them, "Is racing each other a big part of your training? It seems that you wouldn't necessarily need speed for what you do."

"We build strength by racing each other. We need strength," said Najat. From the other end of the table, Gavind was relieved to hear the familiar deep tone in Najat's voice.

"Strength comes from long-distance swimming," countered Palen, "Sometimes we swim the temple lanes for *hours*."

"That's a grand bit of exaggeration!" said Ram. "Anyway, lane laps are for endurance."

"Strength and endurance are the same thing!"

A diver named Vin got back to the question. "We need speed because the destins are fast. We have to be able to catch them."

"Destins aren't fast! They're clumsy!" Palen said.

"A destin can be fast, sometimes!" Vin huffed, defending himself to Jayan. He added a dig at Palen, "*Some* of us have been doing this long enough to know that!"

"He's right," said Ram, cutting his eyes to the Kumasagi. "Najat and I have certainly had our share of chases . . . remember Selda?" Najat snorted into his tea, rolling his eyes.

"You mean Big Selda? You collected *her?!*" Palen laughed. All the divers knew Big Selda. Everyone leaned in to hear more.

Ram prompted Najat, "You tell it."

Najat nodded and set down his cup of tea. But instead of launching into the story, he launched into a brutal coughing fit. The divers all rocked back as if hit by a sudden blast of wind.

"Najat!" cried Jayan, thumping his brother on the back. Najat's upper body shook with each bellowing cough. The pain in his chest caused him to double over, while every thump of Jayan's well-meaning hand drove spikes of fire into his shoulders.

Gavind chewed on his fingernails at the other end of the table.

"Ah-hhham!" Najat rasped, finally signaling the end of his distress. There were tears in his eyes when he lifted his head. Everyone stared at him. "Whoa!" he laughed, sniffing up a suddenly runny nose, "Tea went down the wrong way!"

Most of the divers relaxed, shaking their heads. But Jayan kept his hand on Najat's shoulder. "Are you alright?" the older brother asked in a low voice.

"I'm fine," Najat growled. But then something happened that really startled Jayan. Najat's whole body contracted as if he had been stung by a bug. He uttered a surprised sound, "Huh!" Jayan snatched his hand away as Najat jerked to a straight posture, staring past the divers seated across from him.

Jayan could see that the spot where his brother gazed was empty. He turned back to find Najat's brown eyes glazed over, focused on nothing. "Najat?" Jayan said, afraid to touch him again.

Najat sat frozen, sweat standing at his temples. *Not now . . . not today!* The others would Feel it soon. Jayan's concern turned to confusion as Ram suddenly sat up, getting those same glazed eyes. But Ram wasn't frozen—he started to grin as he looked toward the far wall.

"Ram!!" said Palen, excited. Gavind and Vin were next to snap to attention. Palen and the rest were hit all at once, so that Jayan was left looking around at a table full of glassy eyes and goofy grins. They all seemed to be listening to something that Jayan could not hear.

Suddenly they were all wiping sauce from their fingers and gulping down their last bits of tea. *No!* Najat closed his fists against the familiar, crackling energy that tugged at his heart. Everyone else jumped up from the table and dashed to the window.

"What's going on?" Jayan asked Najat, already rising to follow the others.

Najat shook himself mentally, then conjured up a

pleasant face for his brother's sake. "The Ayudena . . . you can See it from the window. I mean . . . *we* can See it." Jayan didn't hear the last bit, already on his way. Najat remained hunched at the table, wiping his drippy nose and grumbling to himself, "*Crap.*" He did not feel up to the task that lay ahead.

Jayan squirmed in to stand by Ram at the window. They had swung it out and up, propping it with its braces to provide an unobstructed view of Shakti Lake. Jayan saw a beautiful scene before them. Tangled green vines hugged a stand of trees that marched out from directly below them to the shore. The lake glistened like a great crimson gemstone beneath a marvelous blue sky. The diver complex stood on the west shore of the lake. To the north a cluster of billowy clouds rolled serenely toward them. Jayan took it all in, delighting in the fresh breeze that tickled his face.

"There's three shaktis, I think," said Palen, not fully sure of himself. "Right?"

"I count three," said Ram. Vin nodded.

Jayan saw nothing but trees, water, sky, and clouds. Ram was squinting in the direction of those clouds. Jayan squinted, too, but he could not see the Ayudena, or the shaktis.

A booming voice startled him. "*Ai!* What are you little boys gawking at?" They all turned to see a woman of tremendous height and ample girth standing at the top of the stairs with both hands on her hips.

"Big Selda," Palen whispered in Jayan's ear.

"Well, now we're all gawking at the crazy lady," Ram returned her greeting.

"Ha *ha*," Selda growled. Her eyes were busy inspecting each diver—she seemed to be taking a head count. She tilted her chin at Jayan. "Who's this?"

"Ah! Right," said Ram, taking Jayan respectfully by the elbow and steering him to where Selda stood. "Jayan, please meet Selda, First Hand to Amala Tebbe. Selda, *this* . . ." and Ram paused for effect, "is Jayan *Gampoban*."

"Oh!" she said. Her silky gray cheeks lightened to pink as Jayan took her hand.

"Very pleased to meet you," Jayan said, charming her with his rough politeness. The scientific observer in him archived the gray tone of her skin and the silver scales at her wrists—features that characterized the women born from Shakti Lake. Most of the divers were sons of such women, and their coloring was similar. Only Ram had blue-shadowed skin and multicolored wrist scales, marking him as a descendant of Ayunath.

Selda recovered herself. She gripped Jayan's hand in her solid fist and pumped it up and down. "Well, it's my pleasure, my pleasure! I didn't get to meet you the last time you visited!" She did some quick observing of her own, taking in his dark island looks. Jayan's wrists and ankles were patterned with the same golden scales as the Kumasagi's. Selda's eyes found Najat still seated on the floor by the table—she couldn't help glancing from one brother to the other and back. They certainly did resemble each other, only Jayan's hair was thick, fluffy, and cobalt blue, while Najat's head was completely shaved.

Remembering her purpose, she said to Jayan, "I'm sure these fellows have been grand entertainment for you, but you'll have to excuse them for a few hours. I guess you noticed that some shaktis have arrived . . ."

"Yes, so they told me."

Shouts and running feet could be heard from other parts of the building. The cook and two kitchen hands arrived to clear the table—they had to squeeze past Selda to get into the room. They seemed surprised to find the divers still there.

"Right," Selda looked past Jayan and spoke to Ram, "You boys better get your soggy fins down to the dock. Amala Tebbe is already there."

Ram nodded to the other divers, but they needed no prodding. They all rushed to get their sandals on, suddenly hurried and serious. They would have to stop by their apartments and change out of the loose pants they wore to lunch. Ram thanked Jayan for joining them and started to apologize for the hasty departure, but Selda gave the senior diver a gentle push to cut his speech short.

Already on his way out, Gavind glanced back, thinking of Najat. But the divers jostled him down the stairs as Selda herded them from behind. The resulting tide crushed any thoughts he had of turning back.

Only the cook and his helpers noticed that Najat had not moved from the table. When they started to pick up the empty dishes, he shook his head at them and slid his eyes toward Jayan. The cook understood. He bowed to Najat and gestured for the boys to follow him back down the stairs. They could clear the table later.

The brothers were alone. Jayan had wandered back to the window and stood peering across the lake at those same clouds. They were white with purple underbellies, very pretty and well fluffed. Squinting again, Jayan gripped the

31

window frame and leaned so far out that the breeze brushed his hair about his head. Still nothing. They were just clouds.

When he gave up on leaning and straightened, there was a warmth at his back. Najat had silently padded over from the table to stand behind him. Najat did not look out the window himself. He gazed at the floor, taking a moment to focus his mind.

Suddenly Jayan felt Najat's webbed hand pressing into his back. Like the other men, Jayan had not worn a shirt or jacket to lunch. Najat's palm molded over the latent fin ridge between Jayan's bare shoulders, below the back of his neck. The palm radiated with an intense heat, causing Jayan to gasp. The Kumasagi's voice rumbled past his temple, "Look again."

Jayan obeyed, although his physical eyes had not left the vista beyond the window. It took a moment. Najat, half a head taller than his brother, stood patiently with his own eyes closed. His fingertips tightened, denting Jayan's skin. The power flowing from him swept through Jayan's awareness, leaving behind an incredible sense of clarity. The green trees, the red water, the blue sky, and the white clouds leapt unfiltered into Jayan's mind. His breath caught audibly—the shaktis were there. They were not in the clouds after all. Three sparks of light, tiny and colorless at that distance, sank slowly against the clear part of the sky, midway between the clouds and the trees on the northeast horizon.

He looked above the unperturbed clouds and Saw that which had dropped the shaktis. It was The Great Skyfish, Ayudena the Life Giver, swirling and shimmering and gigantic.

Jayan felt his own feet against the floor again, and his breathing returned, heavy and quick. Najat's hand withdrew from his back, taking the Ayudena and shaktis with it. Jayan strained to keep them in sight, but they vanished as he watched. The scenic colors even dulled a bit as his perception returned to its normal state.

His hands felt cramped. Jayan looked down to find himself clutching the window frame hard enough to turn his knuckles yellow. He relaxed his grip, feeling no disappointment. The shaktis were invisible to him again, but he would remember that incredible moment. Jayan was amazed—the Kumasagi must have advanced seriously with his training in the last two years.

Even as his heart swelled with gratitude, Jayan did not turn around to thank his brother. He knew Najat was no longer behind him. Muffled coughs drifted up from the stairwell, each one a bit fainter than the last.

~ CHAPTER 3 ~

The open-air corridor of the seniors' floor bustled with activity as the men dashed back to get changed. Selda waited for Ram, pacing outside his door. Suddenly she heard an excited, familiar voice calling her, "*Ama, Ama!*"

It was her son, a big boy all of three years old, pelting down the planks toward her. He wove around Vin's startled legs and jumped into Selda's arms. "AMA-LA!" he shouted in her ear with his chubby arms around her neck.

She laughed and squeezed him heartily. "What are you doing all the way up here?"

He sat back in her arms and made eye contact. "Did you See the shaktis?"

"Mm-hm," she nodded, "Did you?"

With a dejected pout he looked down and shook his head.

The screen behind them slid open. Ram emerged from his quarters wearing a short skirt wrapped over his diving loincloth. He carried the few other vestments for diving. As he slipped on his sandals, he noticed the boy in Selda's arms.

"Ai, Seldan!" Ram grinned. "What are you doing all the way up here?"

Seldan glowered.

"Uh-oh, what's wrong with him?"

"Ram," Selda enunciated carefully, "How old were *you* when you first Saw a shakti?"

The senior diver scrubbed his chin as they walked toward the stairs. Seldan peeked over at him. Ram gestured an index finger toward the ceiling and said, "I could not See a shakti until I was . . . *sixty-two years old!*"

Seldan was horrified! But then he felt his mother's side shaking beneath him. "Don't let him fool you," she stage-whispered in his ear, "He's not a day over fifty!"

"Ai!" exclaimed Seldan, accusing Ram.

"Ai!" exclaimed Ram, accusing Selda. Ram was, in fact, only twenty-seven years old.

"There he is!" said a voice from the stairway. Two pre-teen boys leapt into the corridor. They bowed to Ram and Selda. "Sorry, Saat. Sorry, Saati," said one, "I don't know how he got all the way up here!"

They received stern looks from both adults—Ram's reminding them that a toddler shouldn't be running underfoot at such a time, and Selda's reminding them that they should take better care of her boy. Seldan was the youngest student at the Diver School.

"I'll hold on to him a little while longer." Big Selda let her face soften, to the boys' relief. She snuggled Seldan to her shoulder as they continued down the stairs. Ram gestured for the boys to follow them outside.

The other divers—all but one—trotted ahead of them down the stone edge of the water lane, toward the dock. The two boys remained a respectful distance behind Selda and Ram. As Seldan bounced contentedly on her hip, Selda took the time to warn the senior diver, "Amala Vengar is also coming. She hadn't arrived yet when I left the dock."

Ram was surprised. "Both Amalas? For just three destins?"

"Yes, and I think they're planning to use all eight divers. They also called for two extra aides from the temple."

"Hmm." Ram added it all up. "That's a boatload, all right. Did Amala say why?" He meant Amala Tebbe.

"It was the Mahasagi. He spoke with her just before I left. Apparently he got an intuition that something . . . might happen."

"Something."

"Right, something, I don't know. I'm not going to question those two!" She laughed.

Seldan squirmed in her arms and smashed his fist into her shoulder for leverage—he was trying to get a better view of the lake as the tree line broke on their left.

"Oof, Seldan!" She set him down on top of the low stone wall that bordered the lane. Ram paused beside Big Selda, and they took a moment to gaze out across the lake at what Selda's son could not yet See. The Ayudena had moved on, but the three shaktis lingered near the north point of the lake, flirting with the surface of the crimson water.

Even those on the dock halted their preparations to witness the shaktis' final descent. They could see no details in the three smudged lights from that distance, but everyone knew enough about the process to project meaning on the fuzzy, miniaturized scene as it played out.

The shaktis themselves were oblivious to being watched—if they were aware of anything, it was not the tiny moving specks on the tiny wooden structure at the far shoreline. From where they hovered, the shaktis could only comprehend the air above and the lake below. Focusing without eyes on a cluster of murky shapes beneath the water, the three arrivals moved with instinct and purpose. The slightly chopped surface of the lake reflected nothing but sky as the glowing spheres drifted apart. One halted, then another, as each aligned herself above a unique heartbeat that only she could feel. It was all done without emotion or thought—each shakti was simply a mass of raw consciousness, naked and mindless, in need of a body.

The third shakti came to a rest just as her sisters began to drop. The two slipped into the lake without any splash or ripple to mark their passing. The third remained in the air a moment longer, alone, waiting as the rhythmic pull from below grew stronger. She pulsed with it, testing it . . . then trembled as velvety waves of heat surged through her, a previously unknown sensation. The promise of greater heat rose from a spot just beneath her. This was the one. Suddenly urgent, she lowered herself toward her newfound destination.

Water and shakti were unaware of each other as the shakti entered the lake. Plantlike shapes loomed about her. She ignored most of them as peripheral objects, not to be touched. Her target was an algae-encrusted pod a few feet below the surface. The pod itself held unmoving at the end of its long stalk, but a sensual energy throbbed forth from inside it to guide the electrified shakti.

Within the ripened vessel, a fully adult female body slept in a curl, suspended in amniotic darkness. The body was not aware of the approaching shakti—it was not even aware that its own thumping heart was a beacon. Its final moments as an empty shell were spent as its first eighteen years had been—incognizant.

Then the shakti arrived, reaching through the crust of the pod to stroke and feel the body. The shakti's final moments as naked energy were cut short by her own crushing need—with a sudden thrust she penetrated the body, shocking it awake. Flesh and limbs responded, trembling as the shakti entered fully. The heat was there, the painfully wonderful heat of rushing blood melting the body and spirit together.

When it was over, the new destin rested. The soft brushing of arms against her legs and the gentle bumping of knees against her chest intrigued her. Slowly her perception settled on something stronger—an unpleasant flavor on her tongue. The fluid in which she floated was also in her mouth and in her lungs and with her new ability to taste she found it repellant. Her eyes blinked open in an effort to understand, but there was no light to help her. The destin kicked and groped in the blackness, elbows knocking against unexpected walls. Tight quarters had never concerned the empty body, but for the newly awakened destin, the walls caused a sudden flush of terror.

Najat Gampoban Felt her panic. Three fingers of dread pressed into his sternum as each of the destins came aware to her claustrophobic prison. He could Feel them all, even as he tried to block them out.

Ram and Selda had moved on. Najat now stood where

they had been, one hand heavy on the stone wall as he looked out across the lake. He had to collect himself before meeting the others on the dock. It had been rash to give Jayan a glimpse of the Ayudena—such a trick required immense effort, regardless of one's health. Najat was aware that he was falling ill, and he intended to hide the fact from everyone else. Yet he had jeopardized his physical condition in that moment with Jayan . . . even now he was not sure why.

He had to get over it. Using the diving vest he carried to mop telltale perspiration from his cheeks, Najat stood squarely and relaxed the soles of his feet against the stone pavers. With a deep, long breath he willed himself to be grounded. Solid. Strong. No coughing allowed. Mercifully, the anxiety projected by the destins faded from his perception.

Finally ready, he turned just as Seldan and the boy's teenaged keepers passed on their way back to the diver complex. The two older boys halted, bowed, and offered the appropriate mudras, making sure Seldan copied their moves. The Kumasagi acknowledged them with a blank nod, already striding along the lane as if he had never paused at all.

As he approached the dock, Najat could see the Mahasagi waiting at the base of the northern ramp—the only way onto the dock from Najat's current position. Najat put on a hurried expression and quickened his pace so that by the time he passed the Mahasagi he was in a fair jog. It was reasonable for him to sweep by with only an abbreviated, apologetic mudra—as the last diver to arrive at the dock he was certainly holding up the whole operation.

Mahasagi Tebhan and his attendants watched Najat with turned heads as he padded up the wooden boards. The old one's First and Second Hands were as tuned to the Kumasagi as they were to their current master. "Mahasagi," whispered the First, touching Tebhan's arm. "He is ill!" Her tone was surprised.

"Yes." The Mahasagi made no move to follow Najat.

"But he can't . . ."

The Mahasagi's eyebrows quirked. "Perhaps he can. It will be interesting to see. If he fails . . ." The Mahasagi's mouth quirked as well, "it could only help our cause, don't you think?"

She shook her head, understanding what he meant but still a bit worried. They could see Najat walking across the dock, his pace much slower now that he had managed to dodge the Mahasagi.

As it turned out, he would be able to dodge Amala Tebbe as well. The dock held two floating barges—for this dive they would take the larger one, which could carry both Amalas. Tebbe already sat in one of two seats raised high above the flat deck of the barge. Najat glanced up at her as he stepped onboard, hoping she wasn't watching for him. She looked frail with her green cloak wrapped up to her neck against the wind. Her withered face gazed forward, oblivious to Najat's late arrival. The Amala was deep in meditation.

Najat noted that the other high seat was still empty. Amala Tebbe's three most senior acolytes were on deck, along with the seven other divers. The oarsmen positioned themselves at the back of the barge. A thick wooden wall split the barge just behind the Amalas' seats, to protect the oarsmen from all that would happen out front.

Ram and the other divers sat on the floor of the barge, quietly facing the lake. They also meditated, clearing their minds with help from soothing energy that emanated from Amala Tebbe. Najat Felt her energy envelope him as well. Big Selda stepped forward and took the vest and other things he carried, setting them aside for the moment as he turned his back to her. She grasped his shoulders, massaging his muscles as he stretched his neck from side to side and flexed his elbows and fingers. Selda's hands magnified the warmth coming from Tebbe. Najat let go of his last troubled thoughts, instinctively beginning the mental procedures that would take him into the proper trance for diving.

The physical part of a diver's task was fairly straightforward. Today three women would be born in Shakti Lake, and it was the divers' job to collect them from the water. Wrestling frightened, flailing destins up onto the barge was arduous work, but each diver's body was prepared after years of training in the Udaka Ruby.

It was the mental aspect of diving that made it difficult and dangerous. Every woman began life as a destin, with a fully matured body and a raw, deficient mind. That mind could only be awakened through a series of initiations from an Amala such as Tebbe. At birth, a destin's instincts would cause her to search for her Amala—but there had been cases of newborn women imprinting on the first person they came into contact with. At Shakti Lake, a destin's first contact would be a diver. Every diver called to serve on the barge must be able to shield him or herself from a destin's grasping energy.

Najat was a master at this. Standing with Selda on the barge, he entered into a calm, well-practiced trance that would make him invisible to the destins. He managed this even as his symptoms from the virus entered a new phase. The pain permeated his stomach now, but it was merely an abstract discomfort because he felt no attachment to it. The method of the trance required Najat to lose attachment to everything, including his sense of self. A destin could not latch onto someone whose mind and spirit were empty.

Najat's awareness was beautifully heightened in this state. He could no longer label the objects around him, and so their properties sprang to his senses unfiltered, intensified. The blue above him deepened, the crimson expanse that lay ahead flashed and bled geometrically. He could Feel the clarity and strength of the divers sitting in front of him, but his disciplined mind had forgotten their names.

Even Selda's hands on his back lost their identity, melting into their own warm contact with his skin. The hands left his shoulders to move past his head and hold up his diving vest. He maneuvered his arms through the holes in the solid front, letting the hands hitch it into place and lace it tightly in the back. The nameless owner of the hands stepped around to face him with his diving sleeves. He slid them on and let the hands tie them securely. They were made from the same rough cloth as the vest, covering his forearms from elbow to wrist.

He stretched again, making sure his bare upper arms were loose. Someone strapped a sheathed pair of surgical clippers around his right thigh. The destins returned to his perception, but their fear only glided through him—for the moment there was nothing in him for it to stick to. He moved to crouch in line with the other men, no longer recognizing them individually but recognizing their purpose together. Every one of them maintained the same trance as Najat. The entire diving operation would be carried out by instinct, without discernment.

The barge had not yet moved from the dock. The divers waited, blankly aware of the sun on their scalps and the breeze against their ears. Not a single thought stirred in any of them when Amala Vengar finally arrived. No one acknowledged the dark-haired beauty as she stepped onto the barge with her three Hands and the two extra aides from the temple.

Vengar climbed the few steps to her seat. The oarsmen in the back could see her head as she settled in on the front side of the wall—both she and Amala Tebbe were positioned to be seen from all areas of the barge. Amala Vengar glanced down over the wall to make sure the oarsmen were ready, then raised her hand as a signal to them.

The barge lurched as the oarsmen pushed off from the dock. Najat's stomach lurched with it, instantly knocking him out of his trance. It was only momentary—he slid back into it easily, as he would a slipped sandal. But the abstract lump in his stomach seemed larger now, more insistent. An odd tingling sensation spiked the fingers of both hands.

Suddenly he Felt the unmistakable, velvety touch of Amala Tebbe's mind. She hovered around him curiously, having noticed a blip among the divers when the barge launched. It was very unusual for the Kumasagi to be distracted out of such a deep meditative state—Tebbe had trained him herself. Najat ignored her as he ignored his hands and ignored his stomach. If he did not acknowledge them, the pain and Amala Tebbe would surely go away.

The barge moved smoothly now, sending a fine mist from the water onto the front deck. The droplets helped protect everyone's skin, which would tend to dry and crack in such a brisk wind. Big Selda and the other attendants worked to prepare large cushions and water-moistened blankets to ease the transport of the destins. The women maintained a trance like the divers, but they did not have to go as deep. After years of living and training with the Amalas, they were adept at blocking the destins mentally.

As the barge approached the north end of the lake, Amala Vengar used hand signals to guide the rowers. Najat's gut swayed in unison with the distant splashing of the oars. His discomfort fell into a rhythm of evolving spasms, building and rising until it seemed to swell against his diaphragm. His only response was to instinctively steady himself with a tingling hand on the deck. He remained blank, not even aware that he was perspiring again.

Praaaack! A sudden, squelching explosion echoed off the midwall. The barge slowed as a patch of bubbled disturbance came into view on the surface of the lake. One of the pods had opened. The divers stood up and removed the skirts from over their loincloths. Najat stood as well and slowly unwound his skirt, as his legs trembled from the effort to stay balanced on the creeping barge. But when the vessel finally halted with a braking lurch, the Kumasagi somehow survived, still standing.

The barge rested a safe distance from the pods so that it

could not drift into their cluster. The Amalas had a good view of the twenty or so egg-like bulbs from their high seats. The divers and others could not see under the water from their lower angle, but they could see the first destin splashing at the surface near the jutting, curled rind of her burst pod. They could not retrieve her yet—they had to wait for the other two pods to open. Ram paced the deck and young Palen stood tensely alert. Amala Vengar had assigned the first destin to them. She did it without verbal commands, instead reaching into the blank mind of each diver to nudge him mentally. Her energy oozed over the other divers, preparing to assign a pair for the second destin.

The second pod exploded underwater, sending a huge bubble to be belched at the surface. Its curled destin shot into the depths of the lake as the mangled pod rebounded off the immature buds around it. The umbilical cord caught the destin, causing her arms and legs to roll open. Back on the barge, the diver Vin watched for her to come to the surface. His pulse raced with a confirmation from Amala Vengar—this destin was his.

On the far side of the cluster, the third pod blew apart with a loud report. Vengar gave a mental tap to Gavind, then moved to signal Najat. The Kumasagi jumped as Vengar's energy tipped into his spine. In that weakened moment, his body could not handle her. He swayed visibly from the effects of his quickening nausea.

Amala Vengar noticed. She motioned to Amala Tebbe, careful not to verbalize her alarm for fear of breaking anyone's trance. Vengar could not deal with Najat—she had to maintain her connection to the other divers. With all three pods open, the water was safe to enter. "Go!" she shouted, the one word that could be spoken as part of the routine. Ram and Palen dove into Shakti Lake.

They swam deftly through the gritty water as Vengar's voice barked distantly behind them with another *Go!* for the second pair of divers. Palen followed Ram with instinctual deference, keeping a vague eye on the senior diver to catch any visual commands. They would not be able to communicate verbally. The cluster of mostly closed, unripened pods came into view, seen by the two divers as a series of blackish purple clumps beneath the red water. Ram cut a wide curve around the left side of the cluster then turned sharply to approach their target head on.

Their destin had stopped splashing. Now she floated stiffly, clinging to a twisted shard from her pod's blown shell. She watched Ram and Palen approach with squinting, sun-shocked eyes. The water around her was turbid with bits of mucus and fleshy plant membrane, and the massive placenta could be seen sagging within the half-submerged pod.

Palen moved quickly, flipping around the destin to grab her from behind. Her skin was slimy and slick, but the rough fabric of his vest helped secure her against his chest. One powerful, sleeved forearm clamped across her sternum, going under her armpits but above her breasts. Palen used the rest of his limbs to tread water as Ram moved in. Before the destin could react, Ram's hands were on her belly, feeling for the umbilical cord. The destin began to scream.

Ram found the cord and compressed it with a clamp produced from a pocket in his vest. The destin struggled, kicking her naked legs at him and beating her arms behind her head at Palen. The two men ignored her, calmly spitting out the water she splashed in their faces and easily deflecting the blows of her weak limbs. Ram unsheathed his pair of clippers from the holster at his thigh and used them to scissor through the umbilical cord. Palen pulled, but a screech of pain from the destin told him that she wasn't yet free. Ram braced a foot against the remains of the pod and briskly clipped off a finger's length of her hair, which had tangled on the pod's jagged rim.

Finally Palen was able to shift her away from the cluster. He kept the destin on her back and moved to take one arm while Ram swam up to grasp the other. She wailed and struggled, but the two divers remained on course, towing her firmly back toward the barge. They passed Vin and another diver who were grappling with their own destin. So far, this had all been routine—the divers in the water were unaware of the crisis unfolding on the deck of the barge.

Gavind poised himself to dive at Vengar's next command. Suddenly two hands closed on his shoulders. Big Selda's voice breathed into his ear, "Not you."

Amala Vengar shouted her signal. The two reserve divers loped past Gavind to dive into the water, heading toward the third destin—the one that had been marked for Gavind and Najat. The junior diver didn't even flinch. He was trained to obey the women on the barge, especially if the decision had Amala Tebbe's energy behind it, as this one did.

To the right of Gavind and Selda, as if he had only been waiting for the rest of the divers to leave, Najat collapsed. He landed on his hands and knees, bringing his stomach with him. The front edge of the deck was close enough to crawl to—he made it there with enough time to position his face over the water and pause. His mind was still clear. Najat began to vomit.

He hadn't eaten much lunch and so he was soon heaving nothing but air and saliva, repeatedly. It was difficult to support himself on his aching hands—the tingling had become a crippling burn, seizing up his muscles. Amala Vengar still lurked inside him, making it all worse. He blasted at her, mindlessly whirling out a barbed, defensive shield. Her energy jumped back as if stung. He shut Tebbe out as well. If no one meddled with him, he could maintain his trance. The Kumasagi's mind remained detached even as his body gasped and choked in its rebellion against the virus.

Selda twisted Gavind so he faced away, but it was too late. The retching noises came in a voice that was unmistakable to Gavind's ears. In that moment of recognition, the junior diver fell out of his own trance. He looked around frantically for Najat, but Selda was a rock behind him, keeping his shoulders squared toward the lake. Suddenly Gavind had another reason to be alarmed—Ram and Palen were approaching the barge with their destin. Gavind tried to slip his mind clear again, but the continuing sounds of distress from Najat tripped him. With rising panic, he sank back against Selda's bosom, needing protection.

"Tch," said Selda. She turned with Gavind, maneuvered him around Najat, and then pushed him toward the side of the deck. "Get off," she commanded in a low tone, so that she wouldn't disturb the other women from their meditation. Gavind obeyed, but only after stealing a glance at the huddled form of the Kumasagi. The cries of the destins reached Gavind's ears as he dove off the barge to swim a safe distance away.

Selda stood over Najat, waiting. He was still incapacitated by his violent stomach, but he seemed to be shielding himself well. The first destin did not notice him. Selda positioned herself to block him visually as the other women moved to the edge of the barge to pull the slippery destin from Ram and Palen's arms. The two divers backed away in the water—they would swim to shore as was the routine. The second pair of divers also delivered their destin without incident—she was tearful and bewildered, as expected for a destin, but she did not pick up on Najat.

It was only when his heaving stopped that Najat fumbled mentally. The sheer relief of getting his breath back again bumped him halfway to normal awareness—a tenuous state to be in as he lifted his head, because at that moment the third destin darted into view. The reserve pair of divers splashed right behind her, having lost their grip for a moment. Najat stared at the destin dumbly, until he saw her staring back at him. She stopped in the water even as the divers caught up to her. At the last moment, she dropped neatly under their reaching hands and disappeared beneath the surface. Najat found himself wondering where she had gone . . . and then he realized he was out of his trance. He caught sight of a pale shape gliding toward him underwater, as ominous as an approaching shark.

Najat tried to scramble backwards and promptly listed to one side, bumping against a solid pair of legs next to him. Big Selda grabbed him under the arms and pulled up just as the destin broke the surface at his feet. The newborn snaked both arms onto the deck and leaned for his buckling legs, but Selda was quick. She dragged Najat back to the middle of the deck as Ram and Palen swam in to help the other divers secure the destin.

This sufficiently agitated the other two newborns, who managed to knock aside the women tending them. The destins both located Najat's unprotected mind and lunged for him bodily. Selda had to shove them away as she stomped past, bringing the stumbling Kumasagi with her to the wall at the middle of the barge. Najat saw Amala Tebbe sitting high above him and felt waves of shame rise with returning nausea. She did not look at him—she was trying to mentally subdue the two wailing destins.

Najat started to fall again, too weak to keep his feet working. Ram and Najat had hauled Selda herself out of the lake only six years earlier—now Selda hauled Najat through the door and into the rowing pit at the back of the barge. The oarsmen stared as she dumped him half gently in the aisle between the benches. On her way back to the door she shot a look at one of the oarsmen, her husband. Then the door slammed behind her as she went back up front to help Tebbe.

Amala Vengar signaled the oarsmen to get the barge moving again, as Selda's husband and another oarsman hurried out of their seats to tend to Najat. They shuffled the Kumasagi to the back of the boat and sat him against a railing. He appeared conscious, but unresponsive. The two oarsmen sat on either side to prop him as he sagged a bit.

Even with his mind clouded and his hands crippled and his lungs and stomach failing him, Najat retained a certain level of pride. He allowed one trembling shoulder to lean against Selda's husband, but he did not let his head or his eyes drop. His line of sight went past the chiseled, cranking arms of the working oarsmen to the blood-toned water beyond. As the barge cut backward on its return across Shakti Lake, Gavind Sandarapan swam as close to it as he could, always staying within Najat's view.

~ CHAPTER 4 ~

Selda returned to a frantic scene at the front deck of the barge. She helped the other women pull the screaming destins away from the door—a door through which the unprotected, tantalizingly naked awareness of a man had disappeared. All three destins were traumatized. It took every ounce of Amala Tebbe's mental will to calm them down, even with Vengar's help.

They still squirmed against the anonymous hands that came to wind up their dangerously long hair and clip it off. The women saved each destin's hair in a separate cloth bag, color-coded to match a cloth band placed around the destin's wrist. They did all this before the barge stopped by the south side of the lake to deposit the Amalas, their attendants, and the destins at a pier connected to the grand Shakti Lake Nursery building.

The women of the nursery transferred the destins to a pool inside the building. The pool water was red, as it was fed by Shakti Lake in the same manner as the Udaka Ruby.

Amala Vengar kept a watchful eye on the destins. Her living quarters were nearby in the east wing of the building, while Amala Tebbe lived in the west wing. Two staircases mirrored each other on opposite sides of the main chamber for easy access by both Amalas and their acolytes.

Under normal circumstances Amala Tebbe would have visited the new batch of destins as well, to see which ones might be drawn to her for *diksha*, their first initiation. But when that particular diving trip ended, the women carried Tebbe immediately up to her apartment and put her into bed. The old Amala had fainted in her seat from the effort it took to restrain the destins.

As Tebbe convalesced, Amala Vengar fumed. The destins showed signs of damage. By the morning after their birth none of them had yet connected with Vengar to begin diksha. She paced by the pool, watching for a spark in any of their eyes, but the destins floated aimlessly, uninterested. "They can't all be waiting for Tebbe!" Vengar said, but only within earshot of her own attendants.

In the afternoon it became apparent that two of the destins were falling ill. "Remove White and Green," Vengar ordered, referring to the destins by the colored tags at their wrists. The nursery acolytes—some of them only a year or two old themselves—waded into the pool and pulled out the two trembling, listless newborns. The acolytes maintained their meditative trance as they bedded down the two destins with cushions and quilts in separate, privacy-screened cubicles.

It was possible that White and Green were simply dehydrated and waning from lack of nourishment—it was rare for a destin to eat between birth and the initial diksha.

But Vengar had her own opinion about the cause of their illness, and she did not bother to keep it to herself. Her angry mutterings reverberated among the women of the nursery as she supervised the treatment of the two destins. Amala Vengar blamed the Kumasagi.

~ * ~ * ~ * ~

A dark skip occurred in Najat's consciousness between watching Gavind from the barge and then waking up in bed. He opened his eyes to calm, filtered light coming through a partially shaded window. The sparsely furnished room was not his own. Najat surmised that he was in the Medical Arts building, part of the temple complex on the south side of the lake.

His next thought was of the Mahasagi. Najat reached out and Found his twin soul several buildings away, in the annex just off the main temple. A familiar twinge in his heart told him that Tebhan was thinking of him as well, waiting for him to wake. The twinge broadened to a steady glow as Tebhan realized that Najat had returned. But it was impossible to tell how Tebhan felt about recent events—the Mahasagi divulged no emotion through the line to Najat. He would share his thoughts when the two saw each other again.

The line dimmed as Tebhan withdrew to give Najat some privacy. Apprehension settled over Najat. There must have been consequences from his recklessness on the barge. He cast out another line and was surprised to Feel Gavind nearby. The junior diver was somewhere on the same floor of the building, in the direction Najat faced as he lay unmoving on his right side. Najat stretched a little further, easily Finding Ram and Vin, but they were both asleep. There was another who felt familiar, whom Najat suddenly sensed was sitting right behind him.

Jayan. With great effort Najat rolled onto his back to look. The movement instantly reasserted the gastralgia and chest pains of his illness. He curled to his other side, facing Jayan with an unsuppressed groan.

"Najat-la!" Once again Jayan's voice came in worried tones, and once again Najat had to endure his brother's icy hand on his fever-flushed shoulder.

Najat steeled himself, then rolled to his back again. "I'm okay," he croaked. The unexpected weight of his own arms surprised him. Every joint in them stung and every muscle ached, yet his arms felt lifeless, immobile.

His bedroll lay on the floor in the center of the room. Jayan crouched on a cushion beside it, hovering over Najat but no longer touching him. "Water?" he offered, lifting a pitcher and cup from a footed tray beside the bed.

Najat nodded but found it difficult to raise himself. Jayan jumped up to procure extra cushions from a storage nook in the wall and then used them to prop Najat into a semi-reclined position. Najat forced his buckling arms to push against the bed, unwilling to let Jayan do all the work, but then his arms trembled so much that he couldn't hold the cup of water, and he had to let Jayan do it for him. The water felt cold on his dry throat.

"It's kind of strange . . ." Jayan said, setting down the empty cup, "I mean, I've never seen you sick like this. Not since Sindhupat, anyway."

"I've never *been* sick," Najat croaked again. Even after the water, his voice was hoarse.

Jayan raised an eyebrow.

"Sindhupat doesn't count," Najat said with as much vehemence as his cracking voice would allow.

"If it makes you feel any better, you weren't the only one to catch this thing."

"Gavind . . ."

"Yes, he's in a bed just down the hall. He was the first one, after you. There must have been something in the lake that day, because all the divers got it . . . the same thing you got."

Najat sank his heavy head back into the cushions. Whatever it was that he "got," he got it before the dive. Najat became aware of stubble on his scalp as it pricked against the cushion's fabric. "Jay. How long has it been since the dive?" he asked.

"It was yesterday. You've been asleep since then." Jayan stood up. "I'm going to let the doctors know you're awake."

He slid the door open and leaned out to signal a nearby nurse. When he returned to the floor next to the bedroll, Najat had another question, "Did they bring the destins back . . . safely? Do you know?"

"Ah, no, I haven't heard much, except that Amala Tebbe has been in bed just as long as you. It's not this," Jayan gestured broadly, indicating Najat's condition. "She was just weak after . . . what happened. They say she's recuperating." He shrugged to show that he had no more information.

Najat's alarm showed on his tense face. "I need to see Selda. Can you get a message to her?"

Jayan nodded as they both heard bustling voices at the doorway. No less than four doctors with a complement of nurses crowded into the room, bowing with mudras toward the Kumasagi. But the commotion was not all for Najat.

"There he is!" A nurse pointed at Jayan. Three of the doctors converged on the surprised explorer, examining him from all sides.

"You don't seem to have a fever," said one, trapping his forehead under her palm.

"Have you had any nausea? Stomach pains?" asked another, denting the flesh below Jayan's rib cage with probing fingers.

The third lifted his right hand. "What's this scratch on your arm? It's infected."

"Ai!" Jayan flinched away, angry.

Najat echoed his protest from the bedroll, "Ai—"

The doctors all snatched their hands behind their backs, but kept Jayan surrounded. The first doctor addressed Jayan more diplomatically, "Saat. Please come with us . . ." She leaned in to explain, lowering her voice so that Najat could not catch the words.

The fourth doctor knelt at Najat's side to commence an examination of him with the help of two nurses. Najat strained to hear the conversation surrounding Jayan. He could see his brother's facial expression change from ruffled suspicion to a neutral stare.

Finally, Jayan looked over to make eye contact with Najat as the three doctors and their aides headed for the door. Jayan moved with them. He threw a few words of reassurance to Najat, "I'll visit again a bit later." Then he was gone.

"Jay?" Najat was left confused.

The remaining doctor offered no explanation. He

distracted Najat by gently pinching the muscles of his arm, sending spidery filaments of pain all the way up to Najat's shoulder blade. The Kumasagi grunted and winced. The doctor nodded to himself and said, "The others have that, too."

One of the nurses took notes as the doctor queried Najat about his additional symptoms, which matched those of the other divers. After finishing his examination, the doctor left the room to let the nurses do their work.

They promptly took care of the necessities. For Najat, who hadn't convalesced for anything since he was a child, having to squat over a bed pot with the help of two women was an extremely discomforting experience. After that was done, the women fed him and gave his head a shave and cleaned up the rest of him. They finished with a gentle application of moisturizing oils to soothe his dry skin—he had been away from water for too long. At the end of it all Najat was wholly exhausted. The nurses set the cushions aside so he could lie flat again, and gathered up their things to leave.

"Wait," Najat stopped the second nurse on her way out. He didn't know if Jayan would make it to the nursery. "Have someone find Selda. Selda Matirajan—Amala Tebbe's First Hand . . . I need to see her." The nurse promised to do so. Najat fell asleep still wondering what had happened with his brother.

Sometime later, a conversation of hushed words seeped into his perception, without disturbing him fully from his deep sleep. "He needs to rest . . ." one voice said softly.

"He'll rest after I'm gone," said a second, familiar voice. Suddenly a hand gripped Najat's shoulder, shaking him. He returned to consciousness with a jolt and blinked his eyes open. Big Selda was leaning over him. One of the nurses stood protesting at the door, but Najat feebly motioned for her to leave.

Selda looked tired in the waning light from the window. She sat on the floor beside Najat and the two studied each other for a moment. Najat spoke first, unable to read her face. "Is Amala all right?"

"She's still recovering. That thing on the barge, it hit her pretty hard." Selda's blunt words made Najat avert his eyes. But then she said, "Listen. All the divers are sick. That trip was doomed no matter what . . . you just happened to be the one who fell first. Did you know, Gavind barely made it back to shore?"

"No, I didn't know."

"Ram and Vin had to drag him like a destin the last half of the way. Then they started feeling it, too."

Najat grunted. This bit of information did not alleviate his guilt.

"So guess what?" Selda had more news for him, "It was Jayan. He gave it to you."

Najat looked at her.

"Well, the bug you got is certainly exotic. They finally figured out that Jayan must've carried it from his last trip. It's some sort of virus."

"Is he okay?" Najat remembered the doctors taking him away.

"Yes, absolutely. They examined him very thoroughly. He's so healthy, I don't know how they know it was him. Makes sense, though. You were the first person he visited when he got into town, and you were the first person to get sick."

"So it's contagious?"

"Not terribly. The divers ate with Jayan, and only the divers got sick. They've also quarantined a few people from the universities where Jayan had visited. Other than that, it seems to be pretty well contained." Her face fell a bit. "Except for the destins, of course . . . I guess it's because their immune system is fragile at this stage . . ."

Najat groaned. He wanted to cover his eyes with his hand but his arms hurt too much to move. Destins were precious assets for the temple, to be protected at all costs. If this batch was ruined, he would never forgive himself.

Selda continued, "Two of them fell ill today. Now, just let me say this: Amala does not blame you. I don't either. But Vengar . . . she was in a rage about the whole thing, and she kind of vented it in your direction."

Najat's face hardened. He did not have to speak his thoughts, as Selda shared his dislike of the younger Amala.

"But the two destins finally went into diksha with her. I think she practically forced it on them. After that she calmed down, because those two are going to be okay."

"Wasn't there a third?"

"Yes, 'Blue'—the healthy one. Still in the pool . . . still *pashi*." Selda meant that the destin was uninitiated. "She won't even look at Vengar. She did eat some food today, amazingly. It's evident that she's meant for our Amala . . . she seems to be waiting. Even Vengar knows it."

"When?"

"I don't know. Amala could probably do it now, if we carried her down there. But the destin seems stable enough, so we're inclined to let Amala keep resting so she can regain as much strength as possible before the diksha."

Najat's concern for Amala Tebbe flared up again. He had not yet checked on her. "Is she awake?" he asked Selda.

Selda's eyes shifted to stare past his shoulder for a moment. "Yes," she smiled, turning her eyes back to Najat, "she's awake."

Holding Selda's gaze, Najat reached out to Tebbe himself. The old Amala's energy greeted him sweetly, cushiony and warm. Selda's presence amplified the connection, so that Najat could almost Feel Tebbe's palm stroke the crown of his head, the gesture of affection she sometimes indulged on him. He didn't mind that Selda was "listening" in—he wanted them both to Feel his apology. Najat closed his eyes and opened his heart, spilling out his regrets to Amala Tebbe.

Her love continued to pulse through him, unwavering. Najat thought she must have misunderstood the message. He was about to try again when Selda's hand on his aching arm stopped him.

"She got it," Selda said, "But it wasn't necessary."

Najat opened his eyes but did not look at Selda. His silence told her that he disagreed. He abruptly severed his line to Amala Tebbe. Selda took her hand from his arm but bit her tongue, not willing to be provoked by his sudden dark mood. She sat as he lay, without movement or speech.

Najat broke the moment himself with a sigh. "I need to rest."

"The nurses wanted to check on you again," Selda said, standing up, "I'll tell them we're done."

She left him with that. When the nurses entered the room a few moments later, Selda did not return with them.

Najat sighed again, knowing he had not deserved a cordial farewell. His mood sank lower as the nurses helped him with the necessities again—this time he had no appetite for the mush they tried to feed him. When they administered a dose of medicine, however, he forced himself to drink it. They said it would help dull the pain in his arms.

The light had faded from the window by the time the nurses tucked him in again. They left a candle burning on the footed tray beside the bed. The Kumasagi did not mind being alone, but he could not sleep. He stared at the ceiling and waited hopelessly for the analgesic to take effect.

The night deepened and the hour grew late. Inside Shakti Lake Nursery, the pashi destin swam in her pool under the calming, soft light of frosted glass lamps. The destin pulled herself out of the water and hunched for a moment over bent legs, then stood up and walked around the pool once, then slipped back into the water and swam again.

One of Amala Vengar's acolytes, a young woman named Fara, sat on a bench near the pool, watching the destin. Fara yawned as the destin came out of the pool and paced around it once again. Another acolyte had come down to share the vigil, but that woman was already asleep on the next bench.

"Fara," someone whispered nearby.

Fara looked around. "Oh, Tez!" she said, also in a whisper.

Her friend Tesame walked quietly to the bench as Fara

yawned again. "Excuse me," said Fara, "Just a little sleepy."

The destin suddenly turned to look at them. Tesame froze. But after gazing at Tesame for a moment, the destin's eyes dropped to the pool and she slipped into the water again.

"It's alright," said Fara, but she still kept her voice low. "She really isn't interested in us. You can maintain the barest shield, and she'll ignore you."

Tesame set down a bucket she was carrying, joined Fara on the bench, and gestured to Vengar's other acolyte. "*She* looks comfortable." The woman was half-stretched and half-slumped on the bench, with both arms and one leg dangling off the side.

Fara chuckled, a bit feebly. "You're here now, so I won't end up like that." Then Fara sat up straight and pinched her own cheeks and stretched back her shoulders. "Right. You're here. How have you been, Tez?"

"Oh, fine!" Tesame and Fara were birth sisters, in the sense that they had both been born from Shakti Lake on the same day. But they had different *dikshanis*—Amala Vengar had initiated Fara, and Amala Tebbe had initiated Tesame. They had been schooled together in their first years, but now they lived in separate wings of the nursery, each in loyal service to her own Amala.

They had remained friends, and so they huddled their heads together now, whispering and catching up. They were close in height and build, and they both wore their white hair pinned up in a double braided bun. Fara's eyes, skin, and scales were a bit darker gray than Tesame's.

"Does Amala Tebbe know that the destin can walk?" Fara asked.

"I don't know . . ." Tesame said. "When did that start?"

"I think she's been doing it since before I got here, around sunset. She hasn't tried to go anywhere . . . she definitely likes to stay near the pool. She's eating, she's walking around . . ." Fara shook her head. "Has a destin ever gone this long before diksha?"

"I think there have been cases. She'll be alright when she meets Amala Tebbe."

"But when—" Fara hushed herself as the destin came out of the pool right next to them and walked up to their bench. Tesame and Fara anchored each other mentally, ready to pull on a full trance if needed. The destin looked at Tesame, then down at the bucket near Tesame's feet. Then the destin turned and walked her way around the pool again.

Tesame relaxed and whispered, "Did you think to put some clothes on her?"

Fara yawned again, then shook her groggy head. "No . . . I mean, she doesn't take well to being touched, for one thing. And she keeps getting back into the water, so . . . it's just easier without . . ."

Tesame gave her a gentle pinch on the arm.

"Right!" Fara said, shaking her head again. "So what's in the bucket? You didn't come from Tebbe's wing."

"No, I was in the grotto."

"Oh, there? Isn't it extremely icky and spooky down there at night?"

"*I* don't think so. I like it there, any time of day or night. I was refilling the lamps." Tesame nudged the bucket with her foot to show her bottle of oil, extra wicks, and cleaning supplies.

"For who? No one is there at night."

64

"It's not for that, it's just . . . a sacred place, right? We should keep it maintained. I don't know why Vengar's crew doesn't go down there as often as we do. I'm going to take you down there sometime."

"Just not after dark, okay?"

"It's a cave—it's always 'dark.' But with the Nakshidra and the lamps, there is enough light down there. Day or night." Tesame reached into the bucket. "I knew you were here, so I brought you some water from the Nakshidra."

She held up a brown ceramic jar with a fitted lid. It was just big enough to cover the palm of her hand. She opened the lid and Fara peered inside.

"Eh," Fara said.

Tesame looked into the jar. "I guess it already faded," she said, disappointed.

"What can you do with it now? You can't drink it."

"Right, that would be very bad!" Tesame laughed.

"Anoint yourself? Or . . . wash your feet with it?"

"*Fara!*" Tesame giggled again.

Suddenly Fara grasped her arm. Tesame looked up to see the destin standing before them. The destin gazed at the jar in Tesame's hand.

"Do you want to see?" Tesame said, and slowly held out the jar.

"Tesame!" Fara whispered.

"It's okay . . ." Tesame held her hand steady as the pashi destin came closer. The destin's own hands rose up to hover and hesitate on either side of Tesame's open palm.

"You can touch it, it's okay," Tesame said.

"Don't let her drink it!" Fara said.

"No, of course . . . that would be bad . . ." Tesame

watched, enthralled, as the destin cupped her hands around the jar and tugged it toward herself. Tesame stood up from the bench to keep her grip on the jar. The destin pulled Tesame's hand and the jar close to her own sternum. Tesame noticed how the destin was taller than herself, as the destin peered down at the small sample of water from the Nakshidra Grotto.

The water in the jar began to glow.

"Tez . . ." said Fara from behind.

Tesame's hand warmed and tingled, and she felt a familiar sense of clarity and serenity envelop her, as she always felt when visiting the Nakshidra Grotto.

"Tez . . . Tesa . . . me . . ." Fara's voice faltered.

The destin smiled. Her teeth, chin, cheeks, and eyes were blue in the light projected from the jar.

Tesame gaped at the destin and wondered at the rejuvenated, glowing liquid in the jar. Then she heard Fara fall to the floor behind her.

"Fara!" Tesame knelt where her friend had slid from the bench. Fara lay in a slump on the tiles, with her head resting on one arm. The destin dropped to her knees beside Tesame, still holding onto Tesame's hand and the jar.

"Fara . . ." Tesame shook her shoulder and touched her mind. Fara resisted her and cuddled further into a deepening, inescapable sleep.

Tesame looked up at the other bench, where Vengar's other acolyte lay splayed and unmoving. "Oh, no . . ." Tesame breathed.

She snatched her hand away from the destin. The jar dropped, but it was a strong little jar and when it hit the tiles it bounced once and then rolled. The Nakshidra water splashed out onto the tiles, clear and oozing and dim.

The destin grunted and scooped her palms into the sticky liquid, trying to hold it, even as its luminescence faded completely.

Tesame crawled backwards, away from the destin, but then the destin snapped her head up, catching Tesame with a cold stare. Tesame quickly summoned the techniques learned from Selda and Amala Tebbe, throwing up a mental shield and letting all emotions and thoughts fall away. But then the destin was beside her, with a wet hand pressed to Tesame's back between the shoulder blades, where the straps of her dress exposed the scant nubs of her latent fin ridge.

Tesame's mind went clear just as the destin locked in with her, coming with her into that empty, transparent space. Tesame could not form any thought to Call out for help, and now she could not even break her own trance, as the destin caught onto it and strengthened it.

Tesame could only stand up, because the destin wanted to stand. They stood for a moment next to the pool. The destin queried herself about the blue water, with her hand still on Tesame's back, and she got the answer from Tesame's memory of visiting the Nakshidra Grotto.

Tesame walked forward, because the destin wanted to walk. They left the pool chamber through a middle door, neither to the west wing nor the east wing. This door led to a shared foyer on the ground floor of the nursery, done up in dark wood and thick carpets. It was a staging room for caretakers of the pashi destins, with linens and supplies kept in good order on the shelves, and cots and cushions for the caretakers to rest.

Tesame and the destin walked around several thick columns of polished wood, which encased some of the support posts for the multilevel nursery building above. They came to a smaller vestibule in a far corner of the room, where oil lamps burned in wall nooks on either side of an ornately carved, solid wood door.

Tesame paused at the closed door. The destin stared at the door and stared at Tesame, perplexed. This is where they needed to go. Tesame had no thought to argue, but it took a moment for her body to recall the habit of taking a key out of her skirt pocket.

With the destin's hand still flattened against the upper ridge of her back, Tesame unlocked the door. They encountered a spiral staircase, familiar to Tesame, but the destin stumbled on the way down. Tesame stumbled with her and sat down hard on the steps.

The destin maintained her footing, but her hand slipped from Tesame's back. It didn't matter to her hold on Tesame's mind. Tesame stood up and continued to blankly lead the destin toward the Nakshidra Grotto.

They continued down a corridor, where pebbled wall nooks held some of the lamps that Tesame had filled earlier. The greater part of the wall was simple dirt and rock, with wooden ribs curving up to support the wall and a wooden roof overhead. The floor was cobblestone, with fallen dirt swept to the side each day by Amala Tebbe's devoted acolytes.

Tesame's sandals shuffled over the stones and the destin's bare feet padded behind her. The tunnel was long. It ran under a water lane near the nursery and then more than halfway under the large park between the nursery and

Shakti Lake Temple.

The walls changed from dirt to brickwork before the tunnel transitioned into a smaller passageway carved from solid rock. Tesame and the destin finally came to another door, even more solid than the first, but much smaller. Oil lamps illuminated tiny mosaics set into the rock all around the door. The images were very old, honoring the Shakti Lake Amalas of previous generations.

Tesame took off her sandals and placed them on a woven mat. She took the same key from her pocket and opened the door without hesitation this time.

The destin swept past Tesame to stand inside the doorway. She saw a dim, bluish light coming from further inside the cave, and she could Feel where the Nakshidra vein trickled and flowed and beckoned to her.

She turned and held Tesame's eyes with her own, one last time. Tesame had led her to a place held most sacred by the acolytes of Amala Tebbe, yet the destin had no understanding of this, and no use for gratitude. Without knowing to be gentle, she released Tesame and let the young woman fall to the floor. Tesame slumped unconscious in a bed of skirts next to the door, as the destin walked on by herself into the grotto.

~ CHAPTER 5 ~

As the candle burned low in Najat's room, the pain in his arms grew maddeningly worse. Sleep would not come to relieve him. He tried to meditate beyond the discomfort, but his mind only stumbled. Frustrated and restless, he succumbed to the half-deranged thought that escaping the bed itself would help.

With a huffed breath and heroic lunge, he used the muscles of his back and thighs to maneuver up to a sitting position.

He remained that way for a moment, bending over his cradled arms. Then, after a quick scramble of legs, he managed to stand up. He teetered from the suddenness of it, but when his feet stayed firm, he realized that his legs were not affected by the virus. He found his center again and took a few shuffling steps around the bedroll, testing this newfound area of strength.

He let his arms fall to his sides and instantly regretted it. Burning blood rushed down into his hands, setting off sharp, snapping sparks in every wrist bone and knuckle. Both hands went into spasms, straining the webbing between his fingers. He folded his arms again to cuddle his hands against his chest, but the spasms continued.

He tried to revive his old self, the one that had a high tolerance for pain. After completely failing at that, he concentrated on walking again. It felt good to move his legs. He made it over to the window just as the candle burned out, flooding the room with darkness.

The scene outside the window jumped to life in sudden contrast. By the lit windows of other buildings and the lamps shining on the lanes below, Najat discovered that he was two stories up on the east side of the Medical Arts building. His view encompassed the nursery off to the left, and the main temple off to the right. The two buildings faced each other across a large, tree-studded park.

Shakti Lake Temple Park included the exterior approach to a sacred cave called the Nakshidra Grotto. Najat could see the boulders surrounding the cave's entrance as a mass of black shapes silhouetted in the dim center of the park.

Najat mulled over those shapes as he cradled his aching hands. He found himself sizing up the distance from the Medical Arts courtyard to the park itself, then across the park to the nebulous black shadows where the cave entrance lay. An ancient grotto sat deep inside the cave, and the luminescent water there was thought to have healing properties. Najat had touched the water himself a few years before, after a mysterious sort of recognition guided him to it. It was like touching bliss.

The doctors in charge of Medical Arts were inclined

toward science, not mysticism, and so they did not keep pitchers of Nakshidra water on hand for their patients. If Najat wanted to soak his hands, he would have to go to the cave himself.

This bit of mindlessness came from a returning fever—it didn't occur to him that anyone would have brought the Kumasagi a bucket of cave water if he only requested it. He surveyed the dark courtyard below, bending his knees gently to test his legs.

No one saw him slip out of his room, then down the hall, down the steps, and out one of the side doors of Medical Arts. Soon he was standing against a patterned mosaic wall near the gate of the courtyard.

He had to rest for a moment because he was trembling again. He wore a pair of loose pants grabbed from the closet on his way out, the only clothing he had found. The night air chilled his lungs, cramping each breath with a torturous rattle. But he would not go back. The park was deserted at such a late hour, and he did not want to miss his opportunity.

Mindful that he was in no condition to swim the lane that ran in front of the courtyard, Najat slipped through the gate and stole along the wall until he found a small bridge to cross. Soon he arrived in the park, where the trees covered his movements.

He found the cave's entrance only after a fair amount of searching among the boulders. His lack of dinner started to affect him along with his crippled hands and a returning fever. There was a narrow metal gate, which he struggled to open—it wasn't locked, but was old and crooked, and the park staff had wedged it tightly closed for the night. Najat pulled on it and squeezed himself through the largest gap he could manage.

He had some trouble on the stairs inside the cave because most of that night's wall candles had burned out hours before, and in the semi-darkness he began to feel dizzy. Najat concentrated on a single thought to keep himself moving: the Nakshidra water would bring him relief.

When he finally staggered into the grotto chamber, he assumed he was alone. He saw the water with its beckoning, eerie light, which pulled him forward on stumbling feet. Najat fell at the lip of the glowing pool and thrust both hands into the soothing, slightly viscous fluid. His body bent and his arms sank until they were immersed above the elbows. He remained that way for a long time, coughing again and shaking, as his hands went numb in the strange water.

Finally his coughing stopped. After the last echo faded off the walls of the chamber, there was a moment of trickling quiet.

Among the trickling, a softer sound drifted near Najat, padding and shuffling from somewhere to his right. He turned his sluggish head, trying to focus. The yellow glow from oil lamps set into crevices around the chamber supplemented the natural blue glow emanating from the water. A form was caught in that odd mixture of light.

It was the form of a woman.

At first this did not alarm Najat, beyond the slight startle at not being alone. Then he registered the fact that the woman was naked. She stood unmoving three armlengths away, watching him. Her white hair had been cropped short, tufting wildly at the top but matted and damp at the bottom, as if she had recently been sitting in water. Najat's eyes dropped from her inquisitive gaze to her breasts, and then to her flat belly, where the crinkled remains of an umbilical cord were still attached. Then he saw that she was not completely naked—a cloth band circled one wrist. Even in that uneven light, he could see that the tag was blue.

Najat jerked back, slinging his numb arms from the pool with an unintentionally artful, airborne arc of glowing water. He realized that it was the pashi destin who stood before him. A dusting of ruby-colored minerals clung to each curve of her gray skin—the same dust that covered any diver when he stepped out of the Udaka Ruby or Shakti Lake.

Najat remembered that the Nakshidra was accessible by an underground tunnel from the nursery. The grotto's spiritual significance was tied in with the lake and the Amalas. Amala Tebbe and her closest acolytes sometimes performed rituals here, but Amala Vengar tended to avoid the place.

He didn't know how this destin had gone unnoticed or how she had managed the journey, but he knew he had to get away from her. She was already moving toward him.

He intended to run, but when he tried to stand up his legs buckled under him. They had been strong enough to get him to the grotto, but now they failed as the fever caught him fully in its grip. Najat felt incredibly tired, too weak to even crawl backwards as the destin approached.

His next reaction was to throw up a mental shield against her, but he couldn't summon enough effort to achieve full invisibility. The destin's attention was not diverted. His distress seemed to fascinate her. She sank to her knees in front of him with the most beautiful expression of concern anyone had ever offered him.

As Najat huffed and strained to keep his fragile shield up, Mahasagi Tebhan arrived in his mind to encourage him. Amala Tebbe weighed in with a command to stay strong. They Knew he was in trouble. They could not communicate with words, but they both flooded Najat with the knowledge that help was coming.

The destin's light gray eyes held him so that he could not close his own or look away. Her aura oozed over him, seeping through cracks in his mental wall even as he tried to keep it between them. In spite of his years of training that told him to resist, he felt himself drawn to her—she emanated a soothing, clarified energy that suggested relief from the virus that consumed him. In Najat's captivated eyes, the destin glowed brighter than the sacred blue water behind her.

"Ah," said the destin, as if greeting him in some strange language of her own. She smiled broadly.

The Kumasagi was disarmed.

His mental wall fell to rubble, effectively crushing the connection to Tebhan and Tebbe. Suddenly the destin's face was intense—Najat's heart and mind were exposed, beautifully strong and deep. Just the right kind for diksha. She leaned so close that he could feel her panting breath on his chin. She was excited.

Najat closed his eyes, slipping in his fevered state toward ecstasy. A series of popping sensations traveled down his sternum as the destin tugged at his life force, the vital *kana* inside of him. With a groan of release, Najat opened himself fully so that she could take it.

Silken waves of heat surged out from his chest to be eagerly absorbed by the glistening destin. He felt her hands on his shoulders. Najat wanted to embrace her, to feel the rest of her body, but his own hands and arms were paralyzed. He embraced her with his heart instead, pulsing with her in shared, exquisite rapture.

His forehead tingled as she narrowed her concentration to his mind. Memories of his childhood flashed by— terrible memories, buried long ago by his own choice. He realized, suddenly and sickeningly, that the destin could See them. The ecstasy ended abruptly as Najat opened his eyes to the destin's hardened face. Her intensity frightened him. He twisted his head to the side, trying to evade her, but she had already locked in. This was why only an Amala could perform diksha.

"*Aaaaugh!*" His scream rumbled off the chamber walls. The destin could See everything. He squirmed against her, feeling his mind bend as she took what she needed.

"Najat!"

The name fell distantly in his ears. He found himself on the attack now, scrambling through the destin's mind in search of her own sense of identity. He would rip it out as she had ripped his out. Suddenly he slipped, carried forward by his own momentum—the destin did not resist him. With an impertinent, sensuous quiver she let his magnificent spirit fall deep within her. Angry, he stabbed a mental claw into the core of her being . . . and felt his own heart crack as if smashed by a boulder. His lungs crumpled—he tried to gasp but couldn't breathe.

"*Najat-la!*" his name came again, louder this time. Amala

Tebbe had arrived. Big Selda carried the Amala on her back like a porter with a loaded basket. "Protect him!" Tebbe ordered, pointing at the trembling Kumasagi.

Selda deposited the Amala at the lip of the grotto and then jumped forward to tear Blue away from Najat. She twisted the destin to face Amala Tebbe, then knelt back to Najat's side, generating a powerful shield of invisibility around him and herself.

The Kumasagi found his breath and cried out again. He was deranged from the pain in his chest, the pain in his head, and also—perversely—from the pain of being separated from Blue. He fought against Selda, but his body was too weak to topple such a fortress. Her shoulder was in his face—frustrated, he bit it. She grunted a curse and slapped the side of his head. Najat let go of her shoulder and sagged in her arms, his dazed brown eyes sparkling with gathering tears.

The destin herself wept in confusion as she looked wildly about for the one whose bond with her had been severed. Amala Tebbe caught her by the arms and tried to hold her still, but Blue's frantic stumbling made it difficult for the Amala to hang on. "Look at me," Tebbe said, attempting to catch the destin's eyes. Blue twisted violently to evade her and immediately lost her balance, crashing against the frail Amala.

Both women fell, but the Amala was saved by the sudden appearance of another woman, who lunged mightily to catch her before she hit the hard stone floor. It was Dechen, the Mahasagi's First Hand. The Mahasagi had sent Dechen and her husband Rajung to retrieve Najat.

Rajung lumbered into the scene to stand over the

crumpled destin. He was a big man with a clear, sharp mind. Both he and Dechen were fully capable of shielding themselves from the destin. Seeing that Blue was unhurt, Rajung picked her up from the floor and forced her to face Amala Tebbe. It was impossible for the sobbing destin to slide out of his iron-fisted grip.

Dechen supported Tebbe from behind. This time the Amala said it as a command: *"Look at me!"* The destin looked. The sobs caught in her throat as her eyes met the Amala's powerful silver gaze. The destin leaned forward with a stunned expression—this tiny, ancient woman emanated the kana that Blue had been seeking. She winced as Amala Tebbe gently opened a line to connect with her torn mind. She had damaged herself as much as she had damaged the man, and the bruises were tender. But she kept still and allowed Tebbe to proceed, instinctively trusting the Amala.

Dechen and Rajung continued to physically support the two women as a sort of amended diksha took place. There was much repair work for Tebbe to do, and it would take more than one session to determine if the destin was salvageable. But the gradually relaxed stance of the destin showed that this initial effort was working.

Selda still crouched with Najat nearby, relieved that the Mahasagi's Hands had arrived to help her mistress. Najat's head drooped against her arm. Selda shook him, determined to keep him conscious. "You can't go out until the Mahasagi takes a look at you," she whispered in his ear. He moaned, still gripped with some inner pain that she couldn't perceive.

It was Rajung's task to carry Najat to Tebhan's quarters

in the temple annex. Rajung cautiously let go of the destin and waited to see if she would break diksha. The destin remained locked in with Amala Tebbe and showed no signs of moving. Satisfied, Rajung slipped to Selda's side and hefted Najat's shivering weight onto his shoulders with her help. Selda pinched Najat's cheeks to keep his eyes open. "I'll go with you," she decided.

They left as Amala Tebbe and the destin continued to gaze at each other, motionless. Dechen watched over the two women as the diksha continued. By the time Selda returned, the Amala had finished. Dechen sat supporting Tebbe's back as Tebbe cradled the destin in her arms—the destin was crying again.

Selda huffed and sat down next to Dechen on the stone lip of the pool. "Can you, uh, help me sneak these two back into the nursery?" she asked. Dechen nodded. It was obvious that neither the Amala nor the destin would be able to walk all the way back without support. The destin sniffled against Tebbe's jutting collarbone.

"How did she get here?" Dechen asked.

"Tesame—one of our acolytes—led her here," Selda replied. "This child put Tesame right under a spell. And two of Vengar's women—they still sleep by the nursery pool."

"Does Vengar know?"

Amala Tebbe shook her head. "Vengar hasn't noticed yet. She was busy with one of her . . . 'guests' tonight, and perhaps already asleep herself."

"Surely she must have Felt it when her acolytes succumbed!"

"I didn't Feel it, myself, when the destin took Tesame." Amala Tebbe's face was full of regrets.

Dechen stared at the destin. "She has that much power?"

"Maybe she did . . . but not anymore," Tebbe said sadly. "And we don't know how this will affect Najat."

"Tebhan is tending to him now."

"We must get back soon, before anyone sees the empty pool," Selda said.

"Can you carry Tesame?" Tebbe asked her.

Selda stretched her shoulders. "That little twig? Of course."

"If we can get her back to the pool, and help those three wake up, then . . . we will have to let them assume that I came down to the pool, and the diksha happened there." Amala Tebbe thought for a moment. "We'll see what Tesame remembers, if anything—it might be best if you take her to her apartment before we let the others wake."

Selda nodded. They both trusted Tesame to keep any knowledge of the incident to herself.

"I'm sure Tesame doesn't know about Najat," Tebbe said. "She, and they—and especially Vengar—should *never* know that Najat was here."

Selda and Dechen agreed.

The destin sniffled again. Selda reached around Dechen to stroke the destin's arm. "Well, Blue," she said, "Everything's okay now?"

"We no longer have to call her Blue," said Amala Tebbe. "Isn't that right?" she spoke to the destin as she might speak to a child.

"You already found your name?" Selda used the same friendly, comforting tones. "What did you two decide?"

Tebbe smiled and gave her newest daughter a tender squeeze. "Her name is Asta."

~ CHAPTER 6 ~

Much to Jayan's relief, the virus turned out to be fairly harmless. It ran its course in each patient without any lasting damage. All of the divers were back on their feet within a few days, except for Najat.

The Kumasagi's convalescence took much longer. His sudden move from Medical Arts to the temple—so quietly in the middle of the night—raised little concern among the medical staff. They found a simple, handwritten note in Najat's empty bed: Mahasagi Tebhan would tend to Najat himself. None of the doctors rushed over to argue. The infectious stage of the illness had passed for Najat, so there was no harm in letting him mend in relative comfort with the Mahasagi.

Only Amala Tebbe, Mahasagi Tebhan, and their loyal Hands knew that the virus was not the reason Najat convalesced.

He remained secluded in the Mahasagi's quarters for many tendays. When anyone tried to visit, Rajung politely turned them away at the door.

Jayan Gampoban spent his mornings at Patal University, assisting the botanists and naturalists as they studied specimens from his latest trip. He spent his afternoons at the bottom of the Mahasagi's staircase, alternately pleading with Rajung and threatening to strangle him. No amount of questioning, bargaining, roaring, or fist shaking worked on Tebhan's unwavering Second Hand. The ever-patient Rajung simply repeated himself as the days wore on, "The Kumasagi still rests. He must not be disturbed."

It was a fair trek from Patal University to the temple complex, which squatted above on the roof of the plateau. One day Jayan started back earlier than usual, electing to hike up the steep southeastern stairpath instead of taking a pedicab up the southern road. He needed the extra time to clear his head before confronting Rajung yet again. Somehow, on this day, he *must* talk his way past the giant oaf to see Najat.

The stairpath bustled with bent porters and weaving message runners—men who spent their lives on foot as Jayan did. It felt good to walk with them. Wide and solid for most of the journey up, the stone steps limped and crumbled at the top, blending with patches of grass at the unofficial service entrance into Shakti Lake City. The entrance was simply a gap where the low eastern and southern walls—also crumbling a bit—did not meet.

Once through the gap, Jayan maneuvered through a sudden swarm of vacant podals and pedicabs. He was even approached by a palanquin team, but he turned down all offers of a ride. He clipped through the crowded open-air market beyond, turning down offers of anything—sweet cakes, scented oils by the jar, canoes for rent. Eventually the market stalls gave way to permanent shops, which then gave way to serene residential streets. The houses increased in size and majesty as Jayan approached the temple complex.

This eastern side of the complex did not have a grand entrance as the south did. Jayan slipped down an alley and emerged at a corner juncture of the temple's water lane. He checked his bearings as he walked along the moss-fissured mosaics that bordered this part of the lane. A shabby old bathhouse—part of Shakti Lake Boys School—stood across the lane on his right. He passed the rear gardens of several more houses on his left, and then the impressively large backside of the Shakti Lake City Aquatic Theater.

A short bridge offered passage to the other side of the lane, where he walked by the school's two lap pools, rolling over in his mind the arguments with which he planned to slay Rajung. His stride lengthened as a small orchard of fruit trees came into view. The trees were part of the Mahasagi's private garden. Jayan was ready. The walk had prepared him. There would be no stopping him this time.

Jayan stopped. In the orchard, slightly obscured by the leaves and white blossoms, an aura of reflected sunlight illuminated the smooth head of a man. Jayan moved to the low wall bordering the orchard to get a closer look. His heart jumped. It was Najat.

Without a thought, Jayan jumped over the wall and ran into the orchard. Najat's slow, contemplative steps followed a path in the opposite direction. "Ai, Najat!" Jayan yelled, but then he caught sight of the Mahasagi off to one side, flanked by Dechen and Rajung. Even at that distance Jayan could see the hint of alarm on their faces as they tracked his sudden appearance. Rajung moved immediately, starting toward him through the trees.

Jayan did not stop, but his sprint skidded down to a hesitant jog when he looked back at his brother. Najat had turned to stare at him. An inexplicable, scale-raising shiver of awe tripped Jayan down further to a walk. Najat stood wrapped and draped in the pale blue robes of a renunciate. It was not normal dress for the Kumasagi—he only wore the robes during sessions of intense mental and spiritual training. Jayan swallowed hard, acutely reminded that his younger brother was an old mystic, older than even their present lifetime.

He continued forward, ignoring Rajung's footsteps and braving Najat's cold posture. But then Najat moved a hand to shade the sun from his eyes, and suddenly his blank expression transformed to surprised recognition. Jayan broke into a run again as Najat's trembling hands reached toward him.

"Jay-la!" Najat's voice trembled a bit as well. He caught his brother's hands between his own palms and bowed to rest his forehead against Jayan's. The ancient gesture caused the scales at Jayan's wrists to flare again, goose bumps following up his arms. It was another reminder . . . Najat could sense the pulse of Jayan's spirit. Jayan could only sense the pulse of a vein in Najat's brow.

Najat pulled back and smiled, but his eyes looked tired. Jayan noticed sharpened angles from cheekbone to ear and jaw to clavicle. "Are you alright?" he asked Najat for the second time in their lives.

"Yes." The word came out with a rasp, scratching the

smile from Najat's lips. He cleared his throat.

"The virus . . . ?"

"No, no." Najat's voice still rasped. "I recovered from that. Soon after they . . . moved me here. But then—" Najat looked over Jayan's shoulder. Jayan turned to see Rajung standing near them.

Najat bent his head toward Rajung and brought his hands up in a mudra of unaffected respect. "Please let me have a moment," he said. Rajung's eyes stayed on Najat, but his head was cocked with an ear toward the Mahasagi. Finally he answered Najat with a silent bow, returning the mudra with great sincerity and then offering the same gesture to Jayan. He stepped backwards with palms pressed to his heart.

Jayan scrubbed absently at his still-prickled arms as he watched Rajung move out of earshot. "But then?" Jayan prompted Najat.

"It's the mantras," Najat said, touching his throat. "Part of training." He paused, thinking. Then: "That is what came after the virus."

"And this?" Jayan swept his hand to indicate Najat's emaciated appearance.

"The training is . . . not easy."

Jayan waited—his brother seemed to be thinking again. Najat gazed at the ground and brushed a hand over his scalp as if to arrange his thoughts.

"Making up for lost time, I suppose," Najat finally said, referring to the Mahasagi. "He couldn't offer the next level of initiations while I was still a diver."

"So you aren't going back. I wondered why they came for your things."

Najat nodded, still watching the grass at his feet. "I'll be with him full time now. He's been wanting it . . . and now I understand why."

"You've been training with him all along—"

"But I couldn't give it my full attention. Not with part of my mind always swimming in the lake." Najat grimaced. His words came up harsh from his scratched throat, "I should have moved over years ago. Now I have to make it up . . ."

"Make up for lost time. Right." Jayan shifted his weight from one foot to the other. He was satisfied—the virus had not harmed Najat. "Well, I have something—some news—to tell you. I was wondering if you'd like to walk out to the wall."

Najat looked up. It was their ritual, at the end of Jayan's visits, to spend a day together walking the perimeter of the plateau. Jayan always revealed the goal of his next expedition during these farewell walks. "Yes, of course," said Najat, disappointed that Jayan would be leaving so soon. He looked back toward the Mahasagi.

"Will they let you?" asked Jayan.

Najat did not answer directly. "I'll have to change out of these robes. Wait here for me." He padded back to where the Mahasagi stood, and Jayan watched the four of them—Najat, Tebhan, Dechen, and Rajung—discuss the idea of Najat going out. They did it without gestures, without emotion. They could have been chatting about the weather.

Najat turned and walked back, absently adjusting the blue cloth across his shoulder. Quirked lips dented one cheek as he reported to Jayan, "He wants me to keep this on."

Another condition for allowing Najat the excursion was that they ride instead of walk. The Mahasagi's private pedicab met them on the street past the theater. As they climbed into the seat, Najat glanced at the early afternoon sun and commented, "We won't have time to make the full circuit."

"We don't need to," Jayan said. He directed the pedaler, "Eastview Teahouse, please."

Najat looked at him, surprised at the change in their routine.

Jayan grinned. "I'll tell you everything when we get there."

The pedicab took them back the way Jayan had walked in, only turning further north. Najat sat quietly watching the houses and trees go by. After a few blocks of this, Jayan—who had never been one to understand silence—broke Najat's reverie with small talk. "Your friend Gavind tried to visit you."

"Yes," Najat said. "You also tried to visit."

"Did Rajung tell you?"

"I . . . Knew. I just couldn't . . ."

"It's alright," said Jayan, alarmed by the increasing gloom of Najat's expression. "Gavind will be happy to see you again." Jayan continued to chat about the divers and their recovery from the virus, and explained how the biologists at the university had singled out a sketch of a yellow-winged fly in one of Jayan's notebooks and how they surmised that it was this insect that passed the virus to Jayan in the first place. He had been bitten several times.

The soliloquy seemed to help—Najat's face relaxed and he nodded as he listened.

One of the doctors from Medical Arts theorized that the scratch on Jayan's arm was the cause of the illness. Jayan had told them the scratch was from a broken branch on a large, thorny bush, and even though he had never seen that kind of plant before, he had forgotten to make a sketch of it. The doctor wondered if the plant was poisonous, but her theory was put down because the contagious aspect of the illness was more consistent with a virus.

Jayan quickly showed Najat the long purple scar on the underside of his right forearm, but then he dropped his arm out of sight and said, "I'm sure it was that yellow fly. The doctors had a grand time with me, trying to fix the fact that I still carried the virus. They gave me sliverbark to induce the symptoms, so the virus would run its course in me, like everyone else. That stuff makes you weak."

"You let them do that?" Najat's eyebrows went up.

"I know . . . I thought my arms would fall off, they hurt so much. But it worked. I was happy to go through it just to get out of there. They had me quarantined for a whole tenday!" Jayan's personality did not sit well in a cage.

He continued, "I didn't get a chance to tell you, but when I was out there near a mountain called Agalagiri, I stumbled on some manmade artifacts and the ruins of several buildings—they looked ancient. It's completely uninhabited out there, so this is . . . I guess it's a new discovery. I finally told Patal University about it after I got out of quarantine."

"Why did you wait to tell them?"

"I couldn't decide who to bring it to. There are politics involved—who gets to send their researchers out there, stake their claim and all that."

"Are you going back there?"

"No!" Jayan said. He cleared his throat. "Someday I might visit again. Both universities are trying to draw up a joint research group. If they can agree on anything, the ruins will be swarming with their archeological teams. As it should be. I'm working with the map makers at Patal to show them the way, and then they can have at it."

The pedicab found the edge of the plateau and followed a wide dirt path along the patchy eastern wall. They passed a few shops and cafes on their approach to the teahouse, as well as a few staring pedestrians. The Mahasagi's elegant pedicab was recognizable. Soon a tail of curious onlookers wagged indiscreetly behind the cab—the locals wondered who was dying.

When the pedicab stopped in front of the Eastview, the escort of gawkers scattered. They peered from behind trees as the owner of the teahouse hurried out to meet the cab. "Ah, Gampoban-Saat!" she said, relieved to recognize Jayan—a regular during the past few tendays—as he stepped down from his seat. Then she saw Najat still sitting in the shadow of the canopy. "Ohhh!" She immediately deduced who he was by his resemblance to Jayan.

"Ai, Suchali," Jayan greeted the woman. He took her arm to belay her excitement and bent to whisper a request in her ear.

She nodded with wide eyes and yelled in no particular direction, "Suchal!"

Her lanky teenaged son ran to her side from within the doorway. She stood on her toes to whisper instructions in his ear and then sent him back inside.

Suchali greeted Najat with reverence as he stepped out

of the cab, "Kumasagi."

He stopped in front of her and pressed his palms together at heart level, bowing slightly with a warm smile. Suchali blushed with pleasure behind her own mudra.

Jayan and Najat followed the tiny woman into her shop, a large open-air café with only a handful of patrons that lazy afternoon. The handful came to their feet and bowed as the Kumasagi walked by. Suchali led the men to the back where a sliding opaque screen opened to a wooden deck. Suchal crouched near the railing, spreading a thin woven mat in front of two plumped cushions. The boy collapsed into a kneeling prostration as Najat stepped onto the boards.

"Ah, no!" said Najat, "Stand, stand!" Suchal obeyed, his eyes lifting from the floor to Najat, then cutting to Jayan and then back to the floor, and then lifting again to steal another glance at each copper-flecked face, comparing them.

"Suchal, the tea!" his mother scolded. "Are you hungry?" she asked her guests as Suchal bolted past her.

While Jayan discussed menu options with Suchali, Najat moved to the edge of the deck where it offered a view over the city's eastern wall. The plateau stepped down from the wall in uneven terraces, pebbled with more shops and houses. A small river traced along the bottom, partially blocked from Najat's view by the staggered roofs and trees.

His eyes wandered over a string of gold-fluted roofs that marked the campus of Patal University. His mind wandered elsewhere. *She* had been in his dream that morning.

Guilt tapped at Najat's throat. Tebhan was exasperated

with Najat's slow recovery from the encounter with Blue. The "training" *was* difficult. Najat felt his throat tighten even further—he had never lied to his brother before that moment in the orchard. There had been no mantras. His vocal chords were splintered from long sessions of screaming, muffled thoughtfully by Rajung with a strong armful of pillows.

"I love this view," said Jayan.

Najat started slightly at his brother's voice. Jayan stood beside him, having finished his menu requests with Suchali. They were alone for the moment.

Najat saw how Jayan's eyes gazed straight ahead, past the houses and shops and the university and the river. His gaze even stepped over the valley beyond. Jayan was looking across to where the valley ended. He was looking at the mountains.

Najat knew this aspect of his brother well.

"Jay . . ."

Jayan looked back at him with that familiar, brightened expression. Najat gripped his arm and steered him to one side of the deck, where the branches of a tall tree reached high enough to shade them.

"Please sit," Najat rasped, folding onto a wooden bench. Tightened fingers around his brother's forearm brought Jayan down with him.

Jayan's hand covered his. "Najat-la, you're shaking." But the shaking stopped at Jayan's words—the Kumasagi had that much control. "Najat—"

"Jay," Najat rushed in with his hoarse voice, "I have to go into retreat. A long retreat. I was hoping that when I'm out . . ." Najat's eyes slid to his knees. "I hope you will come back to Shakti Lake then. This visit wasn't . . . quite . . ."

"Wait, wait!" Jayan laughed. "I'm staying here! That's what I was going to tell *you*!" His laughter was tinged with nervousness—Najat's behavior concerned him. But when Najat looked up he was encouraged to continue, "They offered me a position at Patal. I will teach two geography courses. They're moving my things from your dorm room today!"

Najat stared at him.

"I mean, I accepted the offer!" Jayan tumbled on, "The first course starts two tendays from now. I actually had offers from both, but Patal is the better university, I think. They're giving me an apartment in the faculty quarters. So . . . you can visit me in *my* home!" Jayan laughed again, knowing it was hard to imagine. He had never lived in a place of his own.

Najat was certainly puzzled. "You'll really live here? You'll still be here when I come out of retreat?"

Jayan paused. "How long is your retreat?"

"Thirty and six." Najat said it with resignation, not believing that Jayan could live in one place for a whole year.

"Ah . . . that is a long one." Jayan glanced up at the tree limbs, calculating. "Yes, I'll still be here in a year." He grinned at Najat, who seemed to need reassurance. "I'll be here!"

The blue robes shifted as Najat hunched to rest his head in his hands. His eyes were covered with fingers as his mouth spoke, "I'm glad."

"I should show you where I am at Patal so you can find me next year. Do you want to have lunch there tomorrow? I can come pick you up."

Najat did not answer. He sat unmoving with his face still partially covered.

The pause was too long for Jayan. He repeated, "Tomorrow . . . ?"

The Kumasagi grimaced and pressed one hand to his chest as if he had a pain there. The other hand still hid his eyes as he struggled to speak, "I . . . can't. I'm leaving for the retreat."

"Najat, you—"

"I'm leaving tonight."

"You don't seem well," Jayan blurted.

Najat's shoulders sagged around the hand still at his chest. The curve of his back caught a large patch of sunlight, turning the blue fabric white.

Clinking dishes startled Jayan. Suchal had returned to the mat. Suchali's voice trailed after him, "Only now with the tea? Uf!"

Jayan rose quickly to stand in front of Najat.

Suchali arrived bearing trays of food and set about arranging their meal on the mat as Suchal set out the tea. The boy weathered another scolding for his placement of napkins—he was occupied with stolen glimpses of their famous guests. Jayan stole a glance himself and was relieved to see Najat sitting up again. The Kumasagi gazed toward the back entrance of the teahouse.

"Saat! Saati," Suchali greeted someone at the screen. It was Dechen and Rajung. They returned her greeting kindly but were quick to move across the deck. Rajung positioned himself at Najat's side, and only then did Najat stand up.

"The Mahasagi sends his apologies," Dechen addressed Jayan. "His Eminence is needed at the temple."

"Ohhh!" said Suchali. "Take care of this," she commanded Suchal, pointing at the tray of food. She jumped up to lead Rajung and Najat out through the teahouse. When Jayan moved as well, gentle fingers fell across his wrist.

"Do not follow," Dechen whispered. Her pale green eyes caught and held him. "You will see the Kumasagi again . . . at a better time."

When he tried to move toward the door screen again, her fingers closed firmly around his wrist. She cut her eyes toward the thin back of the boy Suchal, who knelt at the mat with a paused lunch dish in each hand. Suchal stole a quick glance over his shoulder and realized that they were both watching him. He arranged the dishes with a clattering flurry of hands and then hustled back into the teahouse.

Jayan gently but firmly removed Dechen's hand from his arm. "*Now* I know that Najat isn't well enough to be out," he said in low tones. "Why did the Mahasagi let him go with me?"

"It was good for the Kumasagi to see you, as it was good for you to see him. He will be away for a long time."

"But what is *wrong* with him?"

"The Kumasagi's training is difficult, Gampoban-Saat. This is a time of transition for him. But I assure you that he will be well the next time you see him."

"But when will that be?" Jayan said.

Dechen just looked at him.

Jayan scrubbed one hand through his hair and pouted. "I guess I'm not used to being the one who's left behind on the plateau."

"The Kumasagi never felt left behind by you," Dechen

said. She slapped her hands together in a mudra and performed a clipped bow to Jayan. "Be well." Then she turned and walked back into the teahouse.

Jayan stood rooted to the deck as the air fell suddenly quiet. But then he heard a faint crunch of pedicab wheels and ran over to the railing to peer out past the side of the teahouse. He caught a glimpse of the Mahasagi's pedicab, and another that must have brought Dechen and Rajung, as they passed behind the trees on the inside of the eastern wall.

"Guess I'll be walking home, then," he muttered. He returned to the backside of the deck and dropped himself in front of Suchal's sloppily arranged dishes. They overflowed with mounds of fried zucchini and curried potatoes, fish rolls and red fried rice. There was a deep crock of Suchali's famous brown bean casserole, which probably could have served six people.

Jayan held a fish roll in one hand and contemplated Dechen's words. Who was she to know what Najat had ever said or thought? Did she really know Najat that well? Jayan figured he knew his brother just as well or better.

But he had seen them communicate to each other with barely a word or expression. He put the fish roll back down with a grunt. He would never attempt to understand the ways of such mystics, even if his brother was one of them. Najat had been part of that world since the age of nine, when Mahasagi Tebhan recognized the aberration—the only surviving second-born child of their time—as his twin soul and successor. In truth, Najat had been a part of that world for many lifetimes.

Suchal returned to the deck like a silent phantom and

sat down on the furthest bench from Jayan. He waited quietly with his hands wrapped around his knees, until Jayan noticed him and summoned him over.

"You've never seen the Kumasagi before, eh?" Jayan said. "What did you think of him?"

Suchal smiled quickly, but then frowned and crinkled his webbed hands together, as if sensing that it might be a loaded question.

Jayan picked up the fish roll again. "I'm going to have a go at this feast here. I might even have room for a slice of ginger cake, if your ama has it on the menu today."

Suchal nodded but didn't move. His eyes met Jayan's, and for once the boy did not look away. Jayan could see questions brimming in Suchal's eyes—but the questions were not for him.

"We'll see the Kumasagi again," Jayan said.

Suchal cleared his throat. "I'll get your cake."

The boy left the deck while Jayan turned back to his fish roll. He examined the roll from all angles without really seeing it. He thought about the one thing he hadn't had the chance to tell Najat. The reason Jayan was willing to settle at Patal University for a year, or even more, was that he had finally decided to shop for a wife.

~ CHAPTER 7 ~

As the other destins progressed in grooming and training for their moment on the block, Asta waited for the Amalas to decide what to do with her.

She dutifully crafted a braid from the swatches of hair reserved from her birth, weaving in the blue ribbon that previously tagged her wrist. From drawers full of trinkets donated to Shakti Lake Nursery by grieving sons and widowers, she chose a matching set of dull silver clips to secure the ends of her braid. She gave no thought to shining the silver.

The nursery supplied each destin with a fendelwood box to store her braid—Asta's box gathered dust as her sisters were sent to the block and married off one by one.

Amala Vengar took little notice of Asta at first. Her attention was diverted with new destins to be harvested and prepped. But then came a lull—no Ayudena overhead, no destin births. The empty skies reminded Vengar: one braid from the "virus trio" still remained unsold.

"*This* is how she spends her time?" Vengar stood in Asta's empty room, talking to no one in particular although her First Hand stood just beside her. They thumbed through papers stacked on Asta's plain shelves. Each loose page contained a drawing, tightly rendered in pencil or pen and ink.

"Finch, finch, swallow, canary . . . silverback minnow, goldfish, bluefin—these are from the pond in Tebbe's garden. Hmm." Vengar continued her riffling. "A lot of birds and fish . . ."

Several pages remained in one fist as she tossed others onto Asta's desk. Vengar noticed something before it disappeared under the growing pile. She shoved the tussled pages aside to reveal an unfinished piece—a hand with skin and webbing outlined in pencil. The bones of the hand stood out in black ink.

"Anatomy? Ah . . ." Vengar peered down at several thick books on the floor next to the desk. Someone must have brought the books from the medical library. Destins were never permitted to step outside the walls of the nursery and its gardens.

Vengar's First Hand bent to lift the cover of a cloth-hinged folder lying on Asta's bed.

"Don't touch!" Vengar stormed over and seized the portfolio herself to add it with the crinkled stash of drawings under her arm.

She carried the storm all the way to Amala Tebbe's quarters. The old Amala Felt Vengar coming and asked her acolytes to shut the outer doors, but there was no time. Vengar arrived and brushed past the acolytes with her First Hand trotting close behind.

Tebbe sagged back on her divan, disappointed that her foot massage might be cut short. The massages were a sweet blessing for her stiff, aching feet. Vengar always picked an improper time to burst in on her senior colleague.

Vengar burst out now, "That destin of yours. You say she's not fit to show?"

Even as her acolytes stiffened around her, Amala Tebbe maintained a practiced calm. Vengar rarely used pleasant greetings to begin a conversation.

"She is not ready," Tebbe answered. She relaxed further into the warm hands at her feet. The massage had stopped but the hands remained, unmoving.

"You haven't asked *my* opinion," said Vengar.

"Cayman Natarajan has seen the destin and agrees with me. You have not seen the destin. You were unavailable each time we asked."

"Well, then. Shall I offer my opinion based on *this*?" Vengar brandished a fanned handful of drawings.

Amala Tebbe flinched and sucked in her breath—she had to keep herself from verbalizing a sudden pain in both feet. Selda leaned from her position at Tebbe's shoulder to hiss, "*Asta!*"

The massages had been Asta's idea. She could often be found sitting happy and cozy at her beloved Amala's feet. She sat there now—quite unhappy and not at all cozy—with a delicate, aged foot bent under each fist. Asta was frozen by the horrific sight of Vengar's webbed fingers crunching into one of her most detailed black-winged sparrows.

Everyone heard Selda this time. "Asta!"

Asta's eyes fell from her precious drawings and her hands jumped from Tebbe's bent feet to clutch the coverlet instead.

Vengar reached her side in two pouncing steps. "Ah! This is the destin?"

A roomful of silence gave her the answer.

"She's a bit plump," said Vengar. With the drawings returned to her armpit, Vengar bent to brush Asta's white curls aside. "But such a pretty face! Really, if it was just the weight that worried you . . ." Asta's head tilted side to side as directed by Vengar's fingers under her chin. "This isn't a bad one. Some men like them soft, right?"

"Amala Vengar—" said Tebbe.

"Some men would find this one quite attractive."

"Amala—"

"You *know* we've run out of the newer ones," Vengar vented abruptly. "We're showing nothing but the old lot again and again—"

"Amala—"

"Three-year-old rejects—"

"Amala *Vengar!*" said Tebbe. Some of the women in the room were even older than three years. They had chosen life in the temple to be with Amala Tebbe, yet each of them had found herself on the block at some point due to the manipulations of Vengar.

Vengar ran her fingers through Asta's hair as if to sooth the tense atmosphere. "This one would bring a good price. Her talents outweigh whatever shortcomings you've imagined." She bent further to hold the drawings in front of Asta. "You did these, didn't you? They're *very* good! I know Amala Tebbe must be pleased. *I* am *quite* pleased with you."

Asta looked away from her own work in an effort to stay

calm, but she couldn't keep herself from trembling under the continued caress at her scalp. Amala Vengar had very long fingernails.

"Asta! Let's get Amala's feet covered," said Tesame, one of the bolder acolytes after so many years around Big Selda. She rushed in and began fussing with the light blankets, effectively separating Vengar from Asta.

Selda used the opportunity to move in herself. "Asta, we'll let you know when you're needed. Why don't you take these back to your room?" With that, Selda plucked the drawings from Vengar's distracted hands and thrust them at Asta. "Tez . . ."

At the cue, Tesame pulled Asta up to steer her around Vengar and past Vengar's First Hand toward the door. Asta craned her neck to watch Vengar as long as possible, acutely aware of the portfolio still trapped under Vengar's arm.

Selda readjusted the blanket over Tebbe's feet as the room settled again. Vengar recovered herself and sucked in a breath to speak, but Amala Tebbe raised her own voice first. "That destin is *not* ready to be sold. Her development was hampered by the Gampoban Virus. You know she is from that batch."

"*Development?* Have you seen what she can *do*?" Vengar said. "My destins from that batch were sold long ago. This one has even more to offer—here I am, admitting to you that this destin has more value. And the other two fetched very respectable sums!" Vengar chopped the air with her hand to emphasize each word, "A-unique-skill-adds-value! The man who buys her will have something to brag about, even if he has no practical use for her talents."

Pounding footsteps started them all. Asta landed on

spread feet next to Vengar and ripped her portfolio away with such force that its corner left a scratch under the Amala's arm. Vengar's wide eyes met Asta's slivered glare.

"Ai!" yelled Vengar's First Hand as Asta turned to flee. She grabbed Asta's arm and was answered with a cracking slap on the wrist from Asta's other hand. "Ow!" She caught the wide shoulder strap of Asta's halter and this time Asta twirled to smack her solidly in the face. The sound of it reverberated through the stunned room. Asta yanked herself free and bounded out the door with her rescued portfolio.

Vengar's First Hand screamed after her, "*You dare—!*"

The sliding door crashed shut.

The First Hand leapt toward the door but Vengar flung a quick arm to catch her. With a wrenching twist Vengar clamped her First Hand back to her side. The long fingernails dug deep.

Vengar turned, ever so slowly, to face Tebbe and Selda again.

Amala Tebbe rose off the cushions to sit tall against the brewing storm. Her voice did not waver. "Amala Vengar, I apologize. The destin will be reprimanded for this behavior."

Vengar began with a pointed glance at the raked skin under her pale green arm. Then she spoke in rapid, coldly clipped words, "Violence will not be tolerated within these walls. A husband and his family can deal with her 'behavior.' She has a unique talent, so we can skip the domestic training. We will play up the artistic skills and make them the selling point. There will be no difficulty in moving this destin. I would even expect a bidding war, considering the current shortage."

"Amala Vengar, the destin is mute."

Vengar paused at this interjection from Selda. Her eyes cut to Tebbe.

"She cannot speak," Tebbe confirmed. "Communicating with her is a challenge, even for us. Most buyers would consider this an unacceptable flaw."

Vengar's mind chewed on this bit of news. "Is the destin deaf as well?"

There was a cautious pause before Tebbe answered. "No."

"So she is just 'mute . . .'" Vengar kept chewing. "Is there a physical deformity? Or is this the slow development you spoke of?"

Tebbe hesitated.

"It doesn't matter. With our current situation, we can certainly afford to put her out and see if anyone is interested."

"But we have to think of what is best for *her* . . ."

Tesame could hear the Amalas' conversation from where she stood outside the door. She was torn between staying to eavesdrop or going to comfort Asta. Her big heart finally pulled her across the large foyer to where Asta sat huddled against the wall beneath a grand painted mural of the Primordial Amala.

Asta had pushed her drawings into Tesame's hands before sprinting back in to retrieve her portfolio. Tesame returned them now, gently placing them on the portfolio in Asta's lap. The destin trembled with the effort to catch her breath and keep her filled-up eyes from spilling onto the pages.

"That was certainly a bold thing you did," said Tesame.

The good-humored kindness in Tesame's voice triggered a spill after all. Asta covered her face in the crook of one elbow to stifle herself from sobbing.

"Shh . . . shh . . ." Tesame tried to sooth her while keeping a watchful eye on the deserted foyer and Amala Tebbe's closed door.

After a few moments of silent tears, Asta lowered her arm. Her breath returned in a rhythm of sniffles and ragged sighs as she stared down at her drawings and smoothed back the curled corners of the pages with her palms.

"Let's get you back to your room," Tesame said. She moved to help Asta up off the floor but Asta did not move with her. The destin sat with her shoulders curved inward and her hand pressed against her sternum as if she felt a pain there.

Tesame had seen Asta in this pose before. She pulled at her to get her attention. "Asta! Let's go."

Asta let Tesame pull her up, but her shoulders still drooped. She clutched her drawings in both arms as they made their way down a flight of stairs to the second level and the main body of the building.

Unlike most buildings in the temple complex, the main body of the nursery was closed, with no balconies or open corridors for outside access to the rooms. The Amalas' quarters in the west and east wings had ample windows and balconies for their northern view of Shakti Lake, but the square core of the building appeared as a flat-walled fortress, with only three entrances from the outside—one on the lake side for bringing in harvested destins, one on the temple side for visitors and prospective husbands, and the locked door to the grotto tunnel. Asta's room was on the southern side facing the park.

Tesame and Asta arrived to find the room still suffering from Vengar's visit. Asta walked in without even a pause at the door to register the mess. Her eyes were still puffed and red from crying, but they held little emotion now. She went straight to her desk and began sorting through the piles of crushed and not-so-crushed drawings with the clear intention of organizing things back to normal.

Tesame matched Asta's silence and busied herself in other parts of the room. She took Asta's water carafe to be freshened and switched used cups with a clean set. She disappeared for a short while, then returned with a teapot of hot water and enough teabags to restock a little basket on the corner shelf. She prepared a cup, set it to steep on the windowsill, and cranked open the one tiny vertical pane.

Asta looked up as a slight breeze came in to ruffle her pages. It didn't bother her—the reordered stacks were now secure under thin paperweights of slate. She slid the unfinished hand bones into the portfolio with her other anatomy drawings and stashed the whole thing on the top shelf of her wall nook. Only one page remained on her cleared desk—the black-winged sparrow so thoughtlessly crumpled by Vengar. Tesame watched from the window as Asta tried to flatten the wrinkles, but the page was beyond saving.

"Ai," said Tesame.

Asta looked up with a pitiful expression.

"Can I have it?"

Asta shrugged and handed over the drawing.

"Ah, thanks!"

Asta gave a slight snort and a slighter grin, momentarily amused by Tesame's unfeigned gratitude. But her face fell again too quickly.

Tesame scrutinized her for a moment. "Are you . . . going to be okay?"

Asta gazed forward as if the wall had asked the question. She nodded.

Tesame brought the tea from the window. Asta took the cup with another half-smile for Tesame and cocked a thumb toward the west wall behind her. She would take the tea around to her favorite perch.

"You want to go out there?" Tesame said, surprised.

Asta shrugged again as if she had no concern, but when she got to the door she did sneak a quick glance both ways to make sure the corridor was empty.

Tesame tiptoed out with her. They did not have to tiptoe far—Asta's favorite perch was immediately next door to her room. It was a small corner study with nice big windows looking to the south and west.

Tesame dropped her off with a pat on the shoulder. "You'll be alright?"

Asta nodded again.

Tesame believed her. "I'll see you at dinner, then."

Tesame trotted back toward the west wing. She was eager to find out how the Amalas' discussion had finished, if it was finished.

Asta toppled into her favorite cushion near the south window. She felt tired, as if all the emotion had drained from her body and taken her energy with it.

Vengar's latest rant would amount to nothing—surely new destins would arrive to occupy her schedule again. Or perhaps Amala Tebbe would prevail, and Asta would be given another year to "develop." Asta settled further into the cushion and sipped her tea, imagining all the scenarios that would allow her to stay in the nursery.

She liked to sit at this window and watch the courtyard of the Medical Arts building across the lane. Today she saw one patient resting in the sun near the steps and another walking slowly among the flowers with the help of a nurse.

Sparkling movement caught her attention. A halo of sunlit water droplets appeared in the lane that ran in front of the nursery—it was a swimmer, coming steadily from the direction of the library. Asta sat up to get a closer look. This part of the lane was seldom used in the daytime.

The lane ran directly beneath her window before disappearing behind the wall of the nursery's main garden. Even from two stories up, Asta could not see the lane where it hugged the opposite side of that wall. When the swimmer approached, she had few precious seconds to observe who it was.

It was a man. A strong swimmer. When his lifting arms caught the sunlight Asta could see spangled color at his wrists. His blueish skin fell white against the greener blue of the water. Asta's breath caught and quickened—the man's head was shaved bare.

She knew he must be a diver. The garden wall blocked her view of him just as two more arrived in his wake, their arms and legs beating the water in unison. Both had the gray-silver skin of Shakti Lake, the same as Asta's. But they did not have her white hair—they had no hair. Their heads were shaved clean like the head of that first blue diver. Asta's own webbed hand returned to her sternum as the splashing of more divers filtered dimly through the sealed windows.

For endurance training, the divers normally swam the lane on the far side of the park where it ran straight and long in front of the temple and down the far side of Medical Arts. Very rarely—and a lucky day for Asta if she was by the window—they would use the nursery side for its shorter lengths and sharp turns.

She knew about divers, even if she could not read the nursery's textbook lessons very well. Tesame and others had told her plenty about birth (divers retrieve the destins, Amalas perform diksha), and life (marriage and a son, or service in the temple—or sometimes both), and even a little about death (one hopes the Mahasagi will attend).

She knew about men. She had even seen a few men in person. The Mahasagi had visited her with Selda and another kind woman named Dechen. Mahasagi Tebhan was almost as ancient as Amala Tebbe, and had the same silver eyes.

Officials from the temple had come to examine her, and one of them was an extremely tall man with a memorably beakish nose. That happened when she was quite young. The temple sent representatives to inspect every Shakti Lake destin soon after birth.

Even before that meeting, she had seen one other man. It happened in a particularly vivid dream, so this man was not real. But that did not stop her from looking for him among the divers when they happened by under the window. He resembled them, with a shaved head and well-trained swimmer's build.

Asta had grown fond of this imaginary man as the

tendays progressed—that first dream of him was not her last. He always appeared beside her, sometimes more felt than seen.

Asta flushed thinking of it now, as she sat in her cushion by the window watching the last diver pass the wall. Thoughts of this imaginary man always brought on a cavernous feeling in her chest. Clear and open and deep. It felt as if her heart had nothing to beat against.

Asta sat there at the window long after the divers passed. Eventually the lane began to fill again as residents of the plateau came out for a late afternoon swim. A family trio came along slowly, the mother and father keeping a gentle pace for their young son. Soon they were passed by a cluster of older boys who seemed banded together in an effort to distance themselves from their parents. That group of parents came along eventually. Some enjoyed the water themselves and some simply strolled along the edge.

It was time for Asta's own pre-dinner dip in the nursery bath. She left her cushion with no final glances for the outside world. She knew *he* would not be among the families swimming below.

Tesame was not at the bath, and neither did she appear for dinner. In fact, Asta had difficulty finding anyone in the common areas of the west wing. Amala Tebbe's doors were still closed.

Finally Asta ventured up to the blacktop kitchen and received a bowl of lentil soup and some savory flatbread from the old cook. Just as she arrived back down the stairs she heard a familiar raised voice.

It came dimly from across the foyer, further muffled by Amala Tebbe's door. Asta felt a chill right down to the wobbling tray in her hands. Vengar was still in there.

Asta hurried back to her room with the food. She ate her dinner alone, behind her own closed door. She consumed it all in spite of her growing uneasiness over what the Amalas might still be discussing.

It turned out to be an anxious, lonely evening for Asta, but later that night she was compensated. The imaginary man appeared in a new dream, completely different from her previous encounters with him.

In her dream, a sunless sky faded white to the horizon. She couldn't see her own legs through an opaque expanse of wind-chopped gray water. The bottom met her foot. Standing, the surface tickled her ribs. This was a burial lake.

Skeletal remains knocked against her toes and scraped against her ankles. The turbid water hid the jawfish—the carnivorous fish that pick corpses clean. Asta panicked. She struggled toward a spit of dark gray sand ahead. He was there, sitting among black boulders on a rocky, sanded slope above the beach.

She fought the water, pulling her heels from the sucking sand, kicking aside unseen ribs and mandibles, struggling, tiring.

His deep voice rolled through her, "Step out."

She stepped out of the water and met her foot to firm land.

A femur lay sky-white against the charcoal sand. Skeletal piles marked a path up the distant slope to where the man sat.

He stood. A circle of color lay around his bare feet. His eyes were on her—she felt shy in her water-soaked slip, arms crossed over her breasts and belly. The man bent to pick up the thing at his feet—a length of light blue cloth. He carried it down the slope and crossed the beach to her.

It was her first real look at him. His skin, dark bronze with faint, coppery specks. His scales, smooth and golden. His build, tall and slim. His bare feet stopped a short length from hers, his long legs concealed by a wrapped skirt of deep blue silk. His chest and arms were bare, and there was a silver blur around his neck—but his eyes distracted hers. She had never before seen the strange color of his eyes— beautiful, luminous brown eyes. Beautiful lips. A flat, broadly carved nose.

He clutched the blue cloth, hesitating in an awkward pose that provided a sweet contrast to his booming voice.

"Hello." He tried not to boom.

"Hello," she answered with her own voice. The surprise of it made her smile.

He smiled back, a beautiful, wide grin of white teeth and denting cheeks. His arms passed her ears to place the blue cloth around her shoulders. Gently, he adjusted it across the front. He stepped back but his warmth remained with the cloth as it blocked the wind.

"I'm dreaming," she told him.

"Yes," he answered. His grin faded. "I'm . . . not dreaming."

She did not understand. His eyes brushed the sand, then returned to her. He opened his hands toward her right hand, but then hesitated again.

Asta reached out her hand to be accepted between his, and he smiled again, as if she had bestowed a great treasure. Reverently, he brought her palm to meet his chest. He held it there, both webbed hands over her webbed hand, his palms blazing, melting her chilled hand against his sternum. Heat—his skin radiated with heat.

Smiling again, no longer hesitant, he lifted one of his hands to reach toward her.

She leaned closer as his fingers approached her cheek.

A smaller, female hand on Asta's shoulder jarred her awake.

Tesame was kneeling over her. Amala Vengar's pale, mint green face loomed behind Tesame's shoulder. Asta threw an arm across her eyes and groaned.

"I see her vocal chords are functional," came Vengar's voice.

The lingering dream froze to a crisp inside Asta as she remembered the scene from the day before. She knew she was in trouble. She sat up in the bedroll, fully awake but unwilling to lift her eyes from her lap.

The expected torrent did not come. Tesame spoke first.

"So sorry to wake you this early. The Revered Amalas came to a decision last night, about you . . . they're going to give you a chance on the block!" Tesame kept her voice cheerful in the presence of Vengar. "There will be a lot of work, ah . . . to do, so we'll need to get started immedi—ah, today. Soon."

Amala Vengar spoke second, her words slow and careful as if she tiptoed around a poised viper. "I will need to take some of your drawings . . ." Asta could hear the pages being shuffled on the shelves above. "And the portfolio . . ."

Big Selda said nothing. Asta did not even realize Selda was in the room until she looked up to protest the idea of Vengar mangling her work again. Selda's eyes met Asta's and held them while the shuffling continued above and

Asta tried to move the words in her head down to her tongue to protest—to stop Vengar—but of course the same thing happened that always happened when she tried to speak . . . the words lost their way somewhere between her brain and her mouth.

Asta wanted to jump from the bed to stop Vengar by hand, but Selda's fierce gaze restrained her. She communicated her fears to Selda with begging, brimming eyes.

Selda spoke loudly, "Don't worry. Amala Vengar will take good care of your drawings. They'll come back to you without a *single* crease."

Vengar crouched next to Selda in a creepily affable manner and weathered Asta's accusing glare. "We'll keep these pages in the folder, too," Vengar demonstrated for Asta with the portfolio across her knee, "so all will be protected." Vengar's blue eyes crinkled at the corners, spooking Asta. Her long-nailed, stubby fingers stroked the portfolio to reassure the destin. She flipped her black hair over one shoulder and ended the meeting with her typical clipped elocution, "Thank you, my dear. I know you will represent us well. I'll let Selda's team get started. We'll check back in a few days."

The Amala brushed out of the room. Asta was left with Tesame and Selda and an intense need to relieve her bladder. She started crying instead.

Tesame rushed in to hug her and reassure her that it wouldn't be all that bad. If she didn't want a husband, there were ways to sabotage a presentation. If she did want a husband, they would make sure Asta was the prettiest, most interesting and desirable destin on display. They would work it all out.

Asta only half-listened to this consolatory speech. She was thinking of Amala Tebbe—her *dikshani*—her mentor—who had shown such kindness to Asta, and patience, even when Asta failed at the mystic trainings and assessments. Every acolyte who served in the nursery was a mystic. Asta would never know the touch of Tebbe's mind and heart as they did, yet her love for Amala Tebbe matched that of any acolyte.

How could it be that *Vengar* had won the decision over Asta's fate?

~ CHAPTER 8 ~

Big Selda left Asta's room and immediately mobilized a cadre of her own friends to be Asta's prep team. She dispatched the women to examine Asta, while she herself walked across the park to recruit a seamstress from the temple. She knew just the one—an old friend of Amala Tebbe's who had designed Selda's own presentation gown some years before.

Cayman Natarajan and his assistants passed her on their way out the temple's side door. Cayman was the bursar of Shakti Lake Temple, always in the middle of something, but never too distracted to give Amala Tebbe's First Hand a proper mudra of greeting as he passed. Selda displayed a quick mudra in return.

After a productive huddle with the seamstress, Selda returned to the nursery where her prep team stood ready to report. Convening over lunch in the privacy of Selda's day quarters, the women gave their assessment of Asta's physical credits and flaws and outlined their recommendation for a twenty-day grooming regimen. They discussed the fact that the destin couldn't speak, read, or write. Sighing over her plate, Selda recalled that Asta's sisters had been given the basic academic, craftwork, and homecare teachings, but Asta herself had never been invited.

It was late afternoon before Selda returned to Amala Tebbe's quarters—their first chance to confer alone since the exhausting debate with Vengar.

Amala Tebbe's own lunch sat cold and untouched near her hand. She lay on her divan and gazed north, where the room's open screens revealed a gray sky past the balcony.

Selda paced and worried. "If Asta has to go out there, we have to help her in some way. She's got a lot of . . . quirks. We can't let some insensitive oaf get her braid."

Tebbe sat up. "Here, I want to walk, too."

Selda offered an arm for support and slowed her steps to match the old Amala. They circled the room together as Selda continued, "All signs say she should be a mystic, but she's not a mystic. She should be able to talk, but she *won't* talk. She can't read or write—" Selda huffed. "Right, that one is our fault. Maybe we can fix that in time. She'll *need* it."

"And the physical assessments?"

"Her scales are dry, and her hair's a mess, but once we tame that and teach her better oiling habits . . . Amala . . . she's beautiful. You already know it. If we get her fixed up enough, she'll be the only one they notice. But is that what we want?"

Amala Tebbe didn't answer, other than by clutching Selda's arm more heavily as they walked.

"And the drawings," Selda said. "She's talented at *that*. Cayman and Vengar . . . all they need for the sale is her beauty and talent. They won't care who takes her."

"She's *my* daughter. You forget, the destin and her dikshani *do* have a say."

Selda grumbled.

"Selda-la." Tebbe stopped their walking. "Gampoban-Saat is looking for a wife."

"Gampoban . . . ?"

"Jayan Gampoban. Yes."

This surprised Selda, as it surprised everyone else who knew about it. The gritty explorer had long since passed the expected age for buying a wife. His bachelorhood was legendary.

"Maore Natarajan visited me this morning," said Tebbe. "Cayman must have asked her to let it slip—he's certainly agitated over this dry spell. Apparently Cayman heard it from his friends at Patal. Gampo-Saat has been visiting the lower lakes but hasn't found a destin he likes yet—"

"The lower lakes? Cayman must've fallen over when he heard that!"

"Maybe Gampo-Saat is looking for a more . . . earthy woman. In any case, he hasn't found her yet. Maore said that Cayman—she brought their son, by the way . . . extremely well behaved for a toddler—Maore said that Cayman thinks Gampo-Saat is ready to try Shakti Lake."

"Right when we're having a dry spell?!"

Tebbe drew her lips to a line and said nothing.

The context of their conversation dawned on Selda. "No. Not Asta. The Kumasagi . . . if Jayan buys her braid, the Kumasagi will see her again—"

"Mm." Tebbe started their walk again.

"It would destroy him!"

Tebbe shook her head.

"Amala . . ."

"Perhaps I have a little more faith in Najat than you do."

Selda fell silent. Tebbe continued, "After this grueling year—training and working hard to come back to himself, with the Mahasagi guiding him—I know he is doing well. Perhaps such a test will only strengthen him, not destroy him. Let's have a little faith in Tebhan, too!"

"Mm," Selda mumbled.

"Anyway, Jayan Gampoban won't stay in Shakti-Patal. He'll take Asta with him. Najat—and unfortunately you and I since we've grown fond of her—will not see Asta very often here on the plateau."

"You sound like the braid is bought."

"I'm thinking of her. Gampo-Saat is the only match. He would love her drawings—she would be an asset for his travels. She could fill sketchbooks to her heart's content. And he just might have the patience for her communication . . . problems."

"I've heard Jayan Gampoban is *not* a patient man!"

Tebbe hesitated.

"Amala." Now Selda stopped their walk. "You don't know Gampo-Saat any better than I do. Why are you justifying this?"

Tebbe understood what Selda meant. The old one rarely talked things through in such a way. "I need to justify it in my own mind. Against all common sense—at least with regard to Najat—my heart is telling me that this union *should* happen."

"Foresight?"

Tebbe gestured and made a move toward her divan. Maneuvering quickly to support her mistress, Selda helped Tebbe settle back against the pillows.

"May I ask *why* this union should happen?" Selda said.

Tebbe looked out past the balcony to the lake beyond. The water lay heavy and still, darkened to maroon beneath the overcast sky. Tebbe's intense face did not reflect the dull scenery. "The—the island needs her. He will take her there. And their child . . ." *Their child will be a different kind of child.* Tebbe didn't know what any of it meant, but she knew foresight only told of good things.

Selda felt Tebbe's conviction. "Will Tebhan tell Najat?"

"No. Not during his retreat."

"Eh," Selda still felt grumbly. "Does Vengar know about Jayan?"

"She will soon enough."

~ * ~ * ~ * ~

Shakti Lake was truly a last resort for Jayan. Six times in the past year he had met with the Amalas of the three destin lakes in Patal Valley—dubbed the "lower lakes" by those who lived on the plateau above. The valley Amalas treated him graciously, and their nurseries overflowed with new destins to choose from. But none of the women carried the spark that Jayan had always imagined would connect him with his destined mate.

In his youth, Jayan had often listened to the story of his own parents—from various adults of the time, or sometimes even his father. Delan Gampoban had achieved senior status as a Shakti Lake diver before he turned twenty. But then he came down with some kind of affliction, best described as a terrible pain in his chest—or the more sentimental adults would say, "his heart"—which nearly drove him mad. No doctor could help him. He abandoned his position at Shakti Lake and left the plateau altogether in search of someone who would offer him relief. His journey—often embellished in the telling by the more garrulous adults—brought him to Sindhupat Island in the Southern Sea. The people there welcomed him and led him to a cave, where a lone destin had just been born. Delan's heart almost burst at the sight of her, but it was from joy and recognition, instead of pain.

The adults explained to Jayan that a man could sometimes sense a connection to his destined mate, even before she was born. Jayan never forgot the story. Unfortunately, he could not have the same experience with an island-born destin himself. Delan's mate Jeniya, who amazingly bore *two* sons—Jayan and Najat—before she died, had been born from a destin pool that now lay dormant. Not a single pod had grown in that seaside cove, or anywhere else on Sindhupat Island, for more than fifteen years.

The Great Lake of Ayunath also lay dormant. Gahvari and Kandargiri were both productive, but too far away. That left the lower lakes of Patal Valley and Shakti Lake itself as Jayan's only immediate options.

He had hoped to avoid Shakti Lake Nursery. But Jayan finally gave in to the well-meaning pressure of his colleagues at Patal University. They suggested a harmless meeting with representatives from the temple.

Cayman Natarajan himself arrived at Jayan's apartment doorstep on the appointed date, alone, carrying a most gracious smile on his face and a large, flat folder under one arm.

Jayan led the bursar to his sunroom, where wide glass windows offered a lovely view of the eastern valley below the university. The bursar folded his legs onto a cushion across the table from Jayan and set the folder aside. Jayan handed him a cup of strong tea.

"Our extensive catalogue of ready-to-wed destins will surely contain something to your taste," Cayman began.

Jayan wondered if the bursar colored the truth at bit here. Jayan knew that most of Shakti Lake Temple's fresh destins had been sold off several tendays before.

"However," Cayman continued, "I would like to tell you about one destin in particular. We think you would find her most interesting."

"How old is this destin?"

Cayman smiled. "Less than one year since retrieval."

"How does she look?"

Cayman referred to a smaller notebook. "Light gray eyes. Medium-length scale pattern at the wrist and ankle, small pattern at the navel and spinal ridge. Scales are darkened silver with a slight blue tinge. Her skin is light and shades to the cool side." Cayman meant the cool side of gray. "Pale webbing at the fingers and toes. This one's hair contains no streaks. Pure white, with a bit of curl."

Typical. Jayan kept his face politely neutral.

Cayman looked up from his notebook. "Shakti Lake truly produces the *purest* of purebred destins. Only *direct* descendants of women from this lake are permitted to use

it for shedding. We keep very close tabs on the bloodlines."
Cayman said this with unhidden pride, until he noticed
Jayan's dark stare.

"Being a 'half-breed' myself, I am not concerned with
the purity of your stock," Jayan said.

Cayman swallowed. He was a tall man, and some people
thought his large eyes and angular, protruding nose gave
him a comical appearance. But Jayan noticed the
thoughtful calculation in those eyes. Cayman straightened
his spine and looked down at Jayan from across the table.
"My apologies. I believe you can only get a sense of the
destin's appearance, and personal charms, if you attend a
viewing at the nursery."

The bursar placed the folder on the table and untied the
cloth latch. "I had hoped to entice you with *this*." He slid the
folder across to Jayan.

Jayan opened Asta's portfolio and looked inside. His
eyebrows rose as he turned the pages.

"The destin *drew* all of this herself," Cayman said. "She
can do pencils, inks, color—she developed quite a hobby
of it, all on her own." Jayan's reaction pleased him. The
temple staff had removed most of the anatomical
renderings and replaced them with Asta's drawings of birds,
plants, and fish—anything that might pique the interest of
a naturalist.

After a few moments of leafing through the impressive
collection, Jayan allowed Cayman to set the date for a
viewing of the destin. However, Jayan imposed one
condition.

"I would like to see her in a group, if you have enough
destins," he said. "Don't tell me which one did these

drawings."

Cayman smiled. He knew how some men liked to think they were following their intuition when they chose their mate. "Certainly, Gampoban-Saat. And *of course* we have enough destins. Perhaps another will fit your fancy if this one does not."

~ CHAPTER 9 ~

On the appointed date the following tenday, Cayman sent his personal pedicab to gather Jayan from the university. Jayan thought of his brother as he stepped into the cab—it didn't take much to trigger a thought of Najat these days. Jayan had wrangled repeated promises out of Dechen and Rajung over the last year, to insure that he could see Najat immediately upon the Kumasagi's return from his retreat.

The pedicab took Jayan up the switchback road of Marg Shakti and through the massive southern gate into the plateau, where the wall surrounding the top of the plateau stood in much better repair than it did at Jayan's favored—if less impressive—corner entrance. Beyond the southern gate, the inevitable market stalls were also in much better repair than those of the southeast corner market. Jayan knew that the wares at this market demanded a much higher price.

From there the road formed an unbending line straight

north to the temple. At the end of the market, they passed under a free-standing rectangular arch, which marked the beginning of the temple complex. Several generations of mosaic artists had worked on the patterns covering the arch.

Giant buildings loomed immediately past the arch—a balconied pagoda on the left, which housed various dignitaries and other visitors, and the massive Shakti Lake City Waterball Arena on the right. A circular stone plaza— complete with a fountain in the middle—connected the space between the arena and the Shakti Lake City Aquatic Theater.

The pedicab skirted to the right as a long reflecting pool split the road down the middle. Jayan moved over to watch for fish among the landscaped water plants and boulders. He seldom traveled to the complex from this direction, so the giant ornamental carp here were a treat to see. Some of them were as long as his legs. He had helped cultivate one blue-finned variety himself, after carefully bringing several specimens back from Sindhupat Island.

He almost would have preferred to stroll the remaining distance. The fish were probably more interesting than any cut-from-the-mold destin to be offered by Shakti Lake.

Then again, the one destin had actually *drawn* such fish as this. Jayan pondered this as he watched the deep green water. He managed to spot two bluefins before his pedicab reached the temple.

With a nod and a mudra, the pedaler dropped Jayan off where the road formed a wide circle around the end of the reflecting pool. The multistoried wooden balconies of the temple rose before him, capped with a curving red-tiled roof. A long stairway leading up to the entrance undulated with two loosely segregated lines of people climbing up or trotting down.

Cayman did not meet him at the top. A harried temple attendant found Jayan wandering the small front plaza among growing stares from other visitors as they entered or exited the building.

"Natarajan-Saat sends his apologies," the attendant told Jayan. "He has been . . . detained." She paused, as if unsure what to do next. She glanced around the crowd and then looked back at Jayan. Jayan looked back at her.

"Come with me," she said. She led Jayan into the first floor of the temple, which revealed a busy corridor lined with shops—the expensive, upscale kind. Jayan knew the merchants paid well for rent here.

The attendant turned down a narrow side corridor and ushered Jayan into a large room, where a gathering of various son-and-parent configurations sat clustered around low tables. Everyone looked up at Jayan, half of them with full mouths. Jayan noticed the remains of a buffet along one wall. This must be the complimentary lunch provided by the temple for prospective buyers, some of whom had traveled quite far.

The attendant gazed around, trying to find an empty seat for Jayan, while all the guests in the room stared at him, trying to understand his dark complexion. Many of them put down their plates and started to wipe their hands with napkins as they realized who he was. One young man stood up near the back of the room—Jayan recognized him as one of his students. They nodded at each other across the room.

Fierce whispering distracted Jayan from behind.

Another attendant had arrived and seemed to be admonishing the first.

The first attendant turned to Jayan and took his arm. "My apologies, Saat. Please—"

"Saat, please follow us," said the second. They held his arms from either side and herded him from the room. Jayan glanced back to see several people standing halfway up, as if they had hoped to introduce themselves.

Cayman swooped down on them immediately outside the door. "My sincerest apologies, Gampoban-Saat." He took Jayan's arm as the first attendant fell into repeated bows, never lifting her eyes from the floor. Her silvery gray face flushed completely red. Cayman cut his chin at the second, who took the cue and escorted the first attendant away as quickly as possible.

"My apologies," Cayman repeated at least ten times as he hurried Jayan back through the main corridor. "This way." They took a flight of open-air steps to the second floor.

They landed in a large private room, where several attendants stood at attention along mahogany walls. Cayman deposited Jayan at a table in the center and then clapped the fingers and palm of one hand together in a gesture to the waiters.

They all moved at once, bending to lift covers off silver platters and pouring wine into Jayan's glass and scooping food onto his plate. Even the napkin seemed to be made from highest quality linen. One server stood by holding wet minted towels for Jayan to clean his hands with after eating.

Jayan looked at the extravagant spread and wished he could have remained downstairs with the others.

"Ah!" said Cayman. He crossed back to the door to greet someone, "Your Eminence . . ."

Najat? Jayan stood up.

It was not the Kumasagi. A regal, Kandargirian woman with tightly coifed black hair entered the room, causing all the servers to pause and snap into mudra poses with bowed heads.

Jayan brought his hands up as well. He recognized Amala Vengar from stories told by Najat long before. She tipped her head at him but did not return the mudra.

"Gampoban-Saat," she said. "We welcome you to Shakti Lake. We are very pleased, and honored, that you have come to us to find your mate."

Jayan did not say that he had been living in the area for almost a year. He did not say that he doubted Shakti Lake would offer a woman to his taste. It was easier to just say nothing. He nodded his head instead.

It was enough to satisfy Vengar. She returned to the door with Cayman, speaking in low tones. Jayan could hear their conversation perfectly.

"Everyone is *waiting*," she said.

"I know. My apologies. I'll see what I can do."

Vengar left. Jayan could see two acolytes move to flank her as she receded into the corridor. He walked over to stand by Cayman. "She came all the way to the temple to tell you that?"

Cayman gazed into the now empty corridor. "Amala Vengar—Her Eminence—has a habit of . . . showing up in odd places."

The bursar looked away and cleared his throat, as if suddenly aware of his own indiscretion. Jayan smirked. He glanced back at the food and told Cayman, "I'm actually not very hungry. Shall we go across now?"

Cayman bobbed his head. "Certainly. Let us go this way . . ."

He led Jayan downstairs and out one of the smaller back doors. All of the back doors opened to the same expansive wooden deck, where wide steps led down to the lane and the park beyond.

They had bypassed the small shrine area of the temple, which in this Shakti Lake design was almost an afterthought. If one wanted to see glorious, gigantic shrines built to honor Ayudena the Skyfish, the Devadutas, and the Primordial Amala, it was best to travel to the half-deserted city of Old Ayunath.

"If you do find yourself hungry, please let us know at any time," Cayman said as they walked the lane around the park. "Our staff will accommodate you."

Jayan nodded. On the other side of the park they passed the mosaic-detailed wall of the nursery's western garden and came to the core building. It rose four stories above them as a massive, straight-faced cube—a stark visual contrast to the adjoining pagoda-like structures on the left and right. The pagodas seemed to be three stories tall. Jayan knew that the one behind the garden wall on the left housed Amala Tebbe, and the one on the right housed Amala Vengar.

"You've never been inside the nursery, correct?" Cayman said.

"Right."

"It's completely closed to visitors, of course, except for the fourth floor." Cayman led Jayan up a staircase, which

129

stuck out from the center of the cube like a massive, pleated tongue. The steps formed a bridge over the water where the lane hugged the side of the building. A few young men exited from the open double doors with their parents.

The foyer inside bustled with nursery staff and visitors. Cayman gestured toward two small doors to the left and right. "Those lead to the Amalas' wings." He nodded his way past various attendants, then took Jayan up a large stairwell directly across from the front entrance. None of the landings had a window or door.

Sunlight dazzled Jayan's eyes as they emerged onto the fourth floor balcony. Cayman pointed over a stout wooden railing to the park below. "The fourth floor is the only area with balconies in the core section of the nursery," he told Jayan.

An attendant greeted them in the open foyer and took their sandals. Cayman continued his narration as he led Jayan around a corner to walk along the western balcony. The wall to their right contained no doors or windows. "Dressing rooms along here. The other side has one entrance, for the private rooms." Jayan knew that Cayman referred to rooms where a buyer could request a single destin for closer viewing.

Jayan looked down as they passed the top of Amala Tebbe's wing. He could see a flat area of the roof, where the kitchen staff had laid out sections of blackrock to soak in the sun. The heated slabs would be used to cook that night's dinner for Tebbe and her attendants.

Halfway down the length of the building, the wall to their right gave way to a thin railing, which served to separate them from an expansive, open deck area. They had to walk all the way to the end to gain access to the deck, via three ascending wooden steps.

Jayan paused at the higher railing along the north side to absorb an astonishing view of Shakti Lake. He could see the diver complex on the western shore.

"Gampo-Saat," Cayman called to him. Jayan turned to see many eyes upon him. A white canopy shielded the deck from the sun, and several families already occupied the rows of cushions beneath it.

Jayan walked among the gazing eyes to where Cayman stood in the middle aisle. He noticed a few people moving to the back, and wondered if Cayman had ordered them to vacate the now-empty cushions near his feet.

Cayman bent slightly to talk near Jayan's ear. "We could arrange a more private viewing, if you wish."

"*No.*" Jayan said. An attendant arrived to offer him a cup of tea, which—after accepting it with a polite nod—he immediately placed on one of the small tables separating the cushions.

"Very well." Cayman gestured for Jayan to sit, and then folded himself onto the next cushion near the aisle.

"You don't have to—"

"I am here to answer your questions, Gampo-Saat," Cayman said. "I will not reveal anything unless you ask."

"Ai, Gampoban-Saat!" said a voice above them. They both looked up to see Big Selda's smiling face framed by the shadowed underbelly of the canopy.

"Ai!" answered Jayan. He leaned across Cayman to clasp her hand as she knelt down next to them. "Have you heard any word of Najat?"

"Yes! His retreat ended yesterday, and he's already

headed back," she said.

"I thought he was here at the Shakti Lake hut."

"No, the other one. In the valley near Thin River Bend. He only started back this morning." Selda seemed to notice Cayman for the first time as he leaned back to avoid their talking heads. She nodded to him. "Nata-Saat."

"Saati," Cayman said. He remained leaning.

"I need to see him," said Jayan.

"He knows. We'll make sure he finds you." Selda grinned and waggled a thumb between Jayan and the presentation stage. "Don't worry, no one told him about *this* yet. We'll let you tell him."

Jayan cocked his head. "There may be nothing to tell."

Cayman grunted beside him.

"Keep an open mind, Gampo-Saat." Selda smiled and stood up. Above her wrapped skirt of deep red silk, she wore a formal, thin-strapped white top embellished with delicate red and orange embroidery. She adjusted the matching shawl over her shoulder and said, "I have to go back. Good luck."

Jayan watched her walk to the stage and disappear behind the drapery at one side. He noticed for the first time how the mothers seated around him wore formal clothing similar to Selda's. The fathers and sons wore buttoned pants and sleeveless jackets made of silk.

Jayan's drawstring pants were made of linen. He sipped his tea and looked around, failing to spot anyone—other than himself—who had forgotten to wear a shirt or jacket.

The presentation of destins unfolded as formally as the silk clothing of the audience. The long back wall of the dressing rooms provided a backdrop for the stage. A nondescript woman with all the marks of a purebred Shakti Lake daughter mounted the steps to the stage and addressed the audience. "We are pleased to present five destins today, born from the pristine waters of Shakti Lake. We will begin with the visual attributes."

Jayan folded his arms and settled in for the show. Cayman kept his promise and remained silent at Jayan's side.

The first destin wouldn't even raise her eyes. A handler escorted her up the steps to the middle of the stage as the announcer read from prepared notes. "Asta. Diksha performed by Her Eminence Amala Tebbe. Skin: light shade, cool gray. Scales: dark silver. Wrist and ankle: medium pattern. Navel and spine: small pattern."

Jayan thought this sounded like the destin Cayman had described. But she seemed a bit plump, and anyway he couldn't muster much interest toward a destin who only looked at the floor. "Eyes: light gray," said the announcer. The handler whispered something to the destin, but the destin refused to look up.

"This one really does have beautiful eyes," the announcer said as the handler led the destin to the rear of the stage to sit on a cushion. "Just a little shy at the moment."

A different handler escorted a new destin to the stage. This one did look up to steal glances at the crowd. Her face maintained a pretty pink blush as the announcer read her statistics. "Madhurini. Diksha performed by Her Eminence Amala Vengar. Skin: light shade, cool gray. Scales: medium silver. Wrist and ankle: medium pattern. Naval and spine: small pattern."

Jayan sighed. All these destins probably listed the same. He stole a glance at Cayman, but the bursar remained expressionless at his side, watching the stage.

"Eyes: light gray," said the announcer.

The destin, visibly more slim than the first, walked with her handler to sit on the second cushion. The handlers sat behind their respective destins, never allowing them to feel alone.

The remaining handlers and destins took their turn at the center of the stage as the announcer read from her notes. There were some variations. Two of the destins had darker skin with light silver scales visible at the wrists. Another one had yellowish streaks in her hair. All of these destins held their eyes up toward the audience, some with a defiant air. The fifth looked downright angry.

Jayan noticed how the announcer did not mention the destins' ages—normally a crucial statistic for a man to consider when he looked for a mate. Jayan suspected that some of these destins were older than the temple cared to reveal.

After the last destin completed the row in the back of the stage, two new handlers walked up the steps to the front. The first handler stood her destin up and walked her to stand between them. The destin gazed down at the wooden boards of the stage.

"Asta. Diksha performed by Her Eminence Amala Tebbe." The announcer repeated the previous statistics. Then she added new statistics: height, width of bust, width of hips, length of webbing between the fingers. The two handlers on either side of the destin unhooked hidden fasteners at her shoulders and waist to release the front panels of her embroidered, sleeveless overgown. The handlers caught the curving folds of stiff fabric as the panels seemed to peel away from the destin on their own.

Murmurs of appreciation floated up from the crowd.

A low, stiff collar held the back of the overgown in place, as a sort of cape to frame an exposed, sheer undergown. What had previously seemed "plump" now stood revealed as a shapely blend of soft lines and robust, sensual curves.

The lacy, light green fabric of the undergown hung from a fitted border below the destin's collarbone, leaving her shoulders free to the air. The handlers lifted her hands slightly to better show her arms beneath wide, wispy sleeves. The entire piece covered the destin from cleavage to feet, but it did little to conceal her nude body beneath. The cloth fell especially transparent against her breasts and hips, while strategic shadings of green dye added tantalizing shadows to her pubic region.

With deft movements, the two handlers unbuttoned the overgown's collar to allow the third handler to lift the remains of the overgown away, after which they guided the destin in a slow turn until her back faced the audience. More murmurs of appreciation from the crowd. Even Jayan sat up straight. The cloth of the undergown fit nicely along the destin's curves. Shades of green concealed the lower half of her full, perfectly proportioned buttocks, accentuating her hips against the sheer fabric above.

The destin's eyes never left the floor as the two handlers replaced all the panels of her overgown and fastened it into place. Her main handler returned to her side and escorted her across the stage. "Thank you, Tesame," the announcer said. As the pair disappeared behind the drapery at the side of the stage, the next handler brought forward the second destin. "Madhurini," the announcer continued. "Diksha performed by Her Eminence Amala Vengar . . ."

Selda met Tesame and Asta in the long dressing room backstage. They led Asta behind a screened cubicle where other women from the prep team helped them remove Asta's double-layered gown.

"I couldn't get her to look up," Tesame told Selda.

Selda handed a set of undergarments to Asta and let her put them on herself. She lowered her voice, not sure who stood in the cubicles nearby. "We should try to get her to look up at least once. Someone will report it to Amala Vengar otherwise, and we'll all catch it from her before this is over."

Asta looked up.

"Yes, Vengar," Selda said. The women wrapped a long, deep indigo skirt—perfectly tailored to Asta's curves—around Asta's hips and buttoned it in place. It sat low enough to expose the curling pattern of dark scales at her navel.

"Can you look up at the audience at least once?" Tesame asked her. "You can see the lake behind them. Just look out at the lake."

Asta lowered her eyes again. Tesame lifted her own shoulders and shook her head at Selda.

Selda felt a tug in her mind and realized that Amala Tebbe needed her. "Please finish up here," she told the team. "I'll be back shortly."

The team finished dressing Asta without her. They adjusted the bands at Asta's breasts to maximize her cleavage and lowered the midriff top over her head. The top was white, with a low-cut indigo border around her bosom. Sheer sleeves ended in white cuffs just past her elbows, to better show off the scale pattern at her wrists.

They had just finished touching up the paint on her face and pinning her curls in a new configuration when Selda returned to the cubicle. Amala Tebbe walked with a cane beside her.

Asta lifted her eyes and mirrored the deeply respectful mudras of the other women toward the old Amala. Tebbe approached Asta and took her hand.

"Daughter, you look beautiful," Tebbe said.

Asta blushed.

"When you return to the stage, please raise your face and look out at the audience."

Asta narrowed her eyes but turned her hardened look toward the floor instead of Amala Tebbe.

Tebbe squeezed her hand. "You will not gain anything by letting this day pass by you. You must look around yourself. Face your experiences, and you will better understand them."

Once again Asta lifted her eyes to Amala Tebbe. The other women watched the two of them without emitting a sound.

"Yes?" Tebbe said, wiggling Asta's hand a bit with her fingers.

Asta nodded. Tesame let out a sigh, and the other women relaxed.

Back out on the deck, Jayan sat beside Cayman watching the handlers reveal this and that angle of the fifth destin beneath her sheer blue undergown. Jayan's mind wandered back to what lay beneath the undergown of the first destin.

The last destin and handler left the stage, and the announcer proclaimed a short break. Servers walked the rows of cushions to refill empty teacups.

"Do you have any questions so far?" Cayman asked Jayan.

Jayan shook his head.

"Very well. I must leave you for a moment," Cayman said. Then, as an afterthought, "Are you hungry?"

"No, I'm fine."

Cayman bowed his head. "I'll return."

Jayan watched Cayman walk along the aisles to check on the other buyers. Several families stood up to chat with him. All of the sons looked much younger than Jayan.

An attendant walked the central aisle, offering scented and unscented oils to those guests who might need to moisturize their skin. Cayman returned to the cushion beside Jayan as the announcer returned to the stage.

"Please be seated, as we will now tell you more about these lovely destins," the announcer said. The five handlers led their destins back onto the stage from the side wing, and arranged them in a seated row near the back. The destins wore formal clothing now, as a husband might see his wife wear to a ceremonial event.

"Asta," the announcer called the first destin and handler to the center of the stage.

The destin's eyes fluttered back and forth along the floor as she walked beside her handler. Finally, as they stepped into the soft glow where special angled flaps of the canopy filtered sunlight onto the stage, the destin lifted her eyes to the audience.

She took a step back as if the number of faces surprised

her. The handler steadied her with a hand on her elbow. The destin swept a look across the audience and started to drop her eyes again, but then something caught her attention. Her eyes snapped back to one face near the middle aisle.

Jayan saw her looking at him—and saw an expression of recognition burst over her face. Before the announcer could continue, the destin quickly walked forward, following a straight line toward Jayan.

"Asta!" said the handler. The destin checked herself at the edge of the stage and looked around for the steps. She started toward the right side, trying to find her way down to the audience while trying to keep her eyes on the bronze face near the middle.

Jayan stood up, and the rest of the audience followed suit as if in a panic. He could see more handlers emerge from the wings to help the first one corner the destin. They stood with her a moment, whispering to her.

"It's alright," the announcer said to the audience. "Please, remain seated."

The audience folded to their cushions again, murmuring and then shushing each other. Jayan found himself a bit short of breath. He drained his tea as the handlers led the destin back to her cushion. They all remained sitting behind her.

"Ah . . . we'll come back to Asta in a moment," the announcer said. "We can start with our next destin, Madhurini . . ."

The second handler and destin walked to the center of the stage. Cayman leaned over to Jayan and tilted his chin to indicate the first destin, who stared directly at Jayan from the back of the stage.

"That one seems to like you," Cayman said.

Jayan swallowed. "Nata-Saat, which one of these destins produced the drawings that you showed me?"

Cayman smirked. "She did. Asta."

Jayan looked at Cayman. "I think I would like to have some lunch after all, if you don't mind."

"Certainly, Gampo-Saat." Cayman Natarajan's smile broadened, until he was grinning from ear to ear.

~ * ~ * ~ * ~

Later that night, long after the destins had been fed and bathed and sent off to bed, Tesame noticed that Asta's light was still on. She knocked on the door.

Asta cracked open the door, and then opened it wider when she saw Tesame there. She returned to her desk, letting Tesame follow her in.

Tesame sat on a cushion beside Asta as the destin picked up a rag she had been working with. The oil lamp on a shelf above them illuminated a long, open box on the desk. Asta's pashi braid lay in the box. Asta had removed the silver clips from it, and now resumed rubbing the metal with her rag.

Tesame studied her for a moment, then said, "You can talk, can't you?"

Asta kept rubbing. "No," she said.

"No?"

Asta glanced at Tesame. "Sometimes."

"I heard you earlier today."

Asta shrugged and spit into her rag. Her knuckles blurred over the silver, but the metal remained as dull as ever.

"That will never work," Tesame said. "Let me get some polish."

Tesame left the room and returned with a small can of silver polish, a small bottle of wood oil, and a large handful of extra rags. She resumed her seat near Asta and opened the can. "Here you go."

Asta took a small bit of polish and wiped it over the edge of one of the clips. The sliver gleamed back to life. She smiled at Tesame.

"So why are you fixing up your braid?"

The lamplight was bright enough to reveal a sudden blush across Asta's cheeks. She bent over the clips again.

"Never mind, I think I know." Tesame grinned and handed Asta a fresh rag.

Tesame cleaned the fendelwood box with the citrus-scented oil as Asta finished polishing. They pinned each end of the braid with the shining clips and folded it in thirds to fit the length of the box. Tesame replaced the box cover and waved her hand over it, then gave it a final pat.

"For good luck," she said.

Asta snorted. Tesame kissed her forehead and left her with a command, "Now get some sleep!"

As she washed her hands and prepared for bed, Asta thought about the bronze-skinned man with golden scales. She had never considered that he might be a real person until today. Tesame told her he was from a far off, exotic island called Sindhupat.

There must be some connection between them, if he could appear so often in her dreams.

She felt sure that she had seen a look of recognition on

his face. Even during the private viewing after the main presentations, his brown eyes had searched hers with a sort of *knowing*. Asta slipped into bed and thought it funny how the real-life bronze-skinned man had a full head of thick, cobalt blue hair. Dreams could be odd in that way.

When sleep finally claimed her, the man reappeared in her dream, standing tall beside her. She touched his bare shoulder, trying to find his eyes. But his face appeared indistinct, blurring above her against a dusk-purple sky.

His head turned away from her as the dream dissolved into deep, black sleep.

~ CHAPTER 10 ~

As Jayan had done so often before him, Najat sent no word to his brother when he arrived back in Shakti Lake City. After a long bath, a short rest, and an oddly quiet lunch with Tebhan, Najat took the Mahasagi's pedicab to Patal University.

Jayan's morning class had long since ended, and he was at home carrying a box of newly labeled specimen jars to and fro, trying to fit it on any one of his overstuffed shelves. Suddenly—thankfully—the chime sounded at his front door, allowing him to deposit the box on a nearby table and forget about it for the moment.

He opened the door and gaped at the familiar—yet changed—figure that stood before him. "Najat-la!"

Najat laughed, oaken and deep, and embraced Jayan in a strong, heartfelt hug. Jayan felt rebuilt muscles flex along Najat's bare arms and shoulders.

Jayan took a good look at him when they finally pulled apart. Najat smiled again, and his face glowed with returned health. Although he remained on the lean side compared to Jayan, he looked cut enough to challenge the professional waterball players of Shakti Lake City Arena. Today he wore nothing more than an ankle-length wrapped skirt of dark blue silk, brown walking sandals, and a silver torc designed to rest on his shoulders, just around the curve of his neck.

Jayan noticed the four-pronged star of the Kumasagi stamped into the decorative torc. He pointed at Najat's head. "You're still shaving?"

Najat brushed a hand over his bare scalp. He spoke with his familiar resonance, "I'm used to it, I guess. I still swim, even if I'm no longer a diver."

That full voice sounded lovely to Jayan's relieved ears. Najat looked all right—in fact, he looked more fit than Jayan himself. Jayan felt his own joints creak as he slid the door shut behind Najat.

Najat looked at the varied boxes scattered around the front room. Some stood in uneven stacks, already sealed and labeled. Others lay open, surrounded by piles of neatly sectioned twigs, empty jars, and tree leaves pressed dry in folding cards.

"You're leaving?!"

"No, no!" Jayan waved a hand at the piles as if he could shoo them away. "I'm just trying to get things organized. I'll take most of this stuff to the horticulture storehouse." He led Najat into the sunroom and moved a stack of notebooks from the low table.

Najat settled in while Jayan made some tea. "Glad to hear you're not leaving right away. I was afraid I'd missed you."

"Oh, I won't be leaving just yet." Jayan brought the tea,

then folded to sit across from Najat and get another long look at him. "Nice vacation?"

"Not that nice," Najat said. "You'd have to call it a working vacation."

"Was the Mahasagi with you?"

"Not all the time. He came down for a tenday every now and then. The rest of the time he gave me guidance from here."

"I'm looking forward to hearing about it. Will you stay for dinner?"

"I'm sorry," Najat said. He hadn't even touched his tea. "I have an audience with Her Eminence tonight—Amala Tebbe. I just wanted to see you first, even if it's a short visit for today. Maybe you can come to the temple for lunch tomorrow?"

Jayan studied Najat for a moment. "Do you know what's happening tomorrow?"

Najat gazed back at him. "Happening?"

"It's already news, at least on the plateau. They really didn't tell you?"

"Tell me what?"

Jayan clapped his hands together. "That's good! I wanted to tell you myself." He stood up. "Stay there."

Jayan left the room for a moment, and then returned to the table holding a long box in both hands—a box fashioned from smooth, unadorned fendelwood. He opened the rectangular lid and slid the box forward to Najat.

Najat looked inside and found a braid of hair nested against a bed of dark blue silk. His heart skipped a beat, but he didn't know why at first. The braid was pure white, the sign of a Shakti Lake destin. Thin strips of faded blue cloth lined each section of hair. Curving silver clips secured both ends of the braid, and their lovingly polished gleam gave Najat a sudden urge to touch them.

He kept his hands on the table and looked up at Jayan. "You bought a wife?"

Jayan grinned. "Do you believe it?"

Najat considered for a minute, and then broke out a smile of his own. "I believe it. I'm . . . a little surprised that you purchased one from Shakti Lake."

"I know. I actually looked for a long time before finding her. I tried the lower lakes first." Jayan took back the box and fingered the braided hair. "But . . . there was something special about this one."

"Is she Amala Tebbe's or Amala Vengar's?"

Jayan looked up. "Amala Tebbe."

Najat nodded in approval. They both sat there for a moment, soaking in the fact that this not-so-young and heretofore highly independent bachelor had finally bought a braid. "Where is she?" Najat asked.

"Still at the nursery. It took a few days to negotiate everything. I guess they do some kind of handover ceremony—that's tomorrow. And I'm still trying to clean up!" He gestured at the manic splay of boxes and specimen jars. His beloved canoe, old *Swallowtail*, dominated one corner of the room. "But anyway, that's when you can meet her. She's . . . she . . ."

Najat cocked his head and waited.

"She's a bit . . . different. She has some kind of problem with speech."

Najat felt that odd skip in his heartbeat again. He ticked

a finger on the rim of his teacup, but did not drink.

"At *first* they said she can't talk at all—can't speak with words," Jayan said. "So I was able to bargain down the price a bit. Not a lot, because they knew they had me with the drawing thing. She has a skill for drawing things from nature—detailed technical drawings, much better than my own sketches. Anyway, I think the price started low because of the speech problem. But there were other bidders, all from Shakti Lake, and the price suddenly went up." Jayan threw his hands wide and shook his head. "I didn't care— they even tacked on more because I'm not pure from Shakti Lake, but I didn't care. They let me see her a second time. This is when you get to touch them—the destin, I mean—at the second private viewing. So they bring her to me, and we're standing there looking at each other. And of course no one thinks she can talk. Selda Matirajan lifts the destin's hand out to me. I take her hand in my own," Jayan demonstrated with a pantomime, "and suddenly the destin gets this *huge* smile on her face. Teeth showing and everything. Beautiful teeth, by the way. So the destin is smiling, and suddenly she says—looking right into my eyes—she says, 'Hello.'" Jayan let out a great laugh like he'd fooled them all. "Amala Vengar was there and she just about fell *over*! Everyone was shocked! But I couldn't stop grinning at the destin, and she was grinning right back, and she looked so sweet I just wanted to kiss her right there—"

Jayan stopped talking as if an invisible wagging finger had shushed him. Najat appeared to be listening politely. Jayan took a long sip of tea, having just remembered the old stories about second-born sons. According to popular wisdom, Najat was most likely sterile and would have little interest in romantic details. Jayan had never thought to ask Najat about it.

"What is her birth name?" Najat asked.

"Amala Tebbe named her 'Asta.' I probably won't change it."

Najat rubbed his finger along the rim of his cup. "Now that you have a wife . . . will you stay here in Shakti-Patal?"

Jayan laughed. "I haven't thought that far yet." He replaced the fendelwood lid and hugged the box close to his chest. "It all happened as if . . . by fate or something. Remember how Delan and Jeniya met?"

Najat paused, and then nodded.

"It felt like that."

Najat sat back. Their father's precognitive connection with their mother was the stuff of legends. Songs and plays and fantastical novels had been written about it. "How . . . did it happen with you?"

"Everything just fell into place. Right when I started thinking about buying a wife, *both* universities offered me teaching positions near Shakti Lake. When I shopped at the lower lakes anyway, none of the women really fit my taste. Then somehow Cayman heard that I was looking, and he convinced me to try out Shakti Lake, just when this destin—Asta—was put on the block. It was her first time." Jayan studied the wood grain on the lid of the box. "And she seemed to *recognize* me."

"Recognize you?"

"She looked at me as if she had met me before. It's . . . hard to explain."

Najat's fingers drummed the tabletop.

Jayan didn't notice. He gave a chuckle and said, "She's a

bit plump." He made a gesture with both hands. "It's a *curvy* sort of plump. She's really quite beautiful."

"Well, I offer you my sincerest congratulations," said Najat. He stood up.

Jayan jumped up with the box still in hand. "You have to leave?"

"Yes, I must get to that appointment with Amala Tebbe." Najat smiled and gestured for Jayan to lead him back out the front entrance. "And then I do need to rest. Will there be a banquet tomorrow?"

"Yes, here at the university. Some of the professors stepped up for me."

Najat understood. Traditionally the mother and father would hold a wedding banquet for the son in their home.

Najat left his brother at the door with a final fond clasp of hands. "Tomorrow, then."

He nodded to the Mahasagi's trusted pedaler, who had remained outside, and settled into the pedicab. They rolled past several students who had gathered at the curb to gawk. Somewhere between that group of students and the end of the street, Najat's smile fell from his face.

The destin from the Nakshidra Grotto. Najat remembered every moment clearly, up to the point where she penetrated his shattered shield. After that he remembered only pain—deep, inner pain from which it had taken almost a year to rehabilitate.

By what measure could he consider himself soundly cured? On the first day of his return, he had not expected to have thoughts of the destin at all, much less the ridiculous thought that his brother might have purchased her.

149

A destin could have developmental problems if she was disturbed by someone other than an Amala before diksha. That one from the Nakshidra probably became an attendant of Amala Tebbe's, or an aide to one of the cooks. He couldn't imagine that they would try to sell her.

She's a bit . . . different. She has some kind of problem with speech.

Najat scrubbed his brow with stiff fingers. Jayan said his wife-to-be was plump. That sounded nothing like the destin from the Nakshidra. Najat forced his jaw to relax as the pedicab switched back up Shakti Marg and entered the twilit plateau through the southern gate.

The pedaler turned and yelled into the wind, "Did you want to stop at your quarters, Saat?"

"No, the nursery will be fine," Najat yelled back. The pedicab rolled under the walkway that connected the Mahasagi's wing—and Najat's quarters—to the temple, then skirted the park on the east side near the library.

The pedaler dropped Najat off at the corner of the library so he could walk the remaining distance along the water lane, where only foot traffic and swimmers were allowed. A few young boys sat at the edge of the lane, splashing their feet in the water and laughing. They did not recognize the Kumasagi, and offered no mudras as he passed.

As he crossed in front of the nursery, Najat reached a tendril of thought out to Amala Tebbe to let her know of his arrival. Big Selda met him at the far corner of the wall surrounding the gardens on Tebbe's side of the nursery.

She held an oil lamp in one hand, and clasped her other hand to his. "Welcome back!"

"Selda-la," he said. "I never had a chance to apologize for my . . . behavior the last time. I must ask your forgiveness."

She looked at him for a split moment, before her face broke open in understanding. "Ah, you mean when you had the virus! When I visited you in Medical Arts. Right." She clapped him on the back and turned him down a narrow, pebbled path along the garden wall. "You certainly look much improved from that day, I can tell you."

Najat followed the bobbing pool of light from her lamp and contemplated her reply. They came to a wooden door in the wall, where Selda fished a key out of her pocket. Before she could use it, Najat said, "I forgot that you saw me later that night. In the Nakshidra Grotto."

Selda paused.

"I remember certain parts, from before anyone else arrived," Najat said. "Mahasagi told me what happened after. I don't remember it—I don't remember you there. But . . . thank you."

"I serve you as I serve our Amala and Mahasagi," Selda replied. Najat had never heard her use such formal language. She turned her head slightly as if one eye could gauge him more accurately than both. "Mahasagi told *us* that you have fully recovered from the . . . incident."

"Yes. I have," Najat said. Selda's eye bored into him, and he found himself raising a shield between that eye and his heart. She would start to wonder about it, if she sensed him shielding—and he barely knew why he did it himself—so he also raised his chin and threw out a verbal distraction: "Mahasagi never told me what happened to that destin. Was she all right?"

Selda turned back to the door and rattled the key in the

lock. "Amala Tebbe knows more about it. That destin was hers."

She led Najat into the garden, where the fading purple sky revealed ornamental fish ponds, interesting rock formations, and an abundance of exotic shrubs and flowers—many of them cultivated from Jayan Gampoban's specimens. Najat followed Selda into the terraced building that served as Amala Tebbe's residence. Most of the Amala's attendants lived on the lower levels. Selda and Najat took the open-air staircase to the third level, where a large foyer led to the grand doors of Tebbe's apartment.

Selda knocked once and then entered with Najat at her heels. Tebbe's sunlit essence enveloped Najat before he even saw her. He looked to her usual spot on the divan, but it lay empty. This evening Tebbe had chosen to sit in a low, cushioned chair near the balcony, wrapped comfortably in her robes and yellow shawl. Najat stepped forward and knelt to one knee on the ornate rug before her, his silver collar glinting under the candlelight.

"Najat-la," she said with smiling silver eyes. She smoothed back the skin of his scalp with one soft hand. A warm sensation oozed down his neck and into his shoulders, relaxing his muscles along the way.

He took her hand—so tiny against his long, webbed fingers—and closed his own hands over it, opening his kana to her. Her wizened face broke into a smile to match her eyes. "Ah," she said. "Tebhan told me you have done well with your studies."

Najat replaced her hand in her lap and gave it a pat. Then he clasped his hands on his knee and looked up at her. "I just returned from visiting Jayan."

Tebbe settled back in the chair. "Did he have some news for you?"

"Yes. He told me he has purchased a wife."

His own words caused a stir in his heart again. He tried to clamp it down, but sitting right in front of Tebbe made it difficult to hide his thoughts. He sensed a hint of mint and the weighted smell of iron, and realized that Dechen and Rajung had just walked into the room behind him. They said nothing, not even a greeting for Tebbe and Selda. Dechen sat down on the floor beside Najat, and Rajung followed suit with a noticeable creaking of floorboards.

Mahasagi Tebhan himself appeared next to Rajung. He stood for a moment to let Najat register his presence, then bent to sit on a cushion across from Najat. Tebhan's tendons sounded as creaky as the floorboards as he settled his legs into a comfortable position.

Najat looked back at Selda, but she simply sat down on the floor beside Tebbe's chair. Najat looked up at Tebbe. She gazed down at him kindly, almost . . . apologetically?

Najat began to understand, as he looked around the circle of concerned eyes, all watching him. He traded a long stare with Tebhan, then said, "You all knew that Jayan has purchased a wife."

Tebhan nodded.

"And . . . you all know who his wife is."

Tebhan, Dechen, Rajung, Selda, and Amala Tebbe all nodded.

Najat looked back at them, and it felt as if his heart could not decide whether to rise or sink. It made his chest hurt terribly. He realized now, without a doubt, that Jayan had purchased Blue, the destin from the Nakshidra Grotto.

~ CHAPTER 11 ~

Under normal circumstances, Cayman Natarajan would conduct the final transaction for the purchase of a destin in his own office on the second floor of the temple. The client would then proceed across the park to collect his destin from the nursery and pay his respects to her Amala. The couple's first appearance on the front steps of the nursery could be formally witnessed by anyone—usually the client's parents, a small gathering of friends, and perhaps a few curious onlookers.

When the widely known and well respected Jayan Gampoban chose a destin from Shakti Lake, Cayman did not even think of treating such an opportunity as normal circumstances.

He postponed all appointments with other buyers, and sent out message runners and avian message fliers to trumpet the news across Shakti Lake City, down the plateau, and deep into Patal Valley itself. Within two days the verbal grapevine reversed to a tangible migration of well-wishers converging toward the top of the plateau. Cayman declared a holiday, opened the park to all permit-bearing entertainers and vendors, and let his assistants take care of the rest.

He met Jayan on the open-aired fourth floor of the nursery, rather than in the temple office. Tradition held that the final transaction must be a private discussion between the bursar and client. A few members of the nursery and temple staff stood a respectful distance away as Jayan carried his fendelwood box up to the grand stage, where Cayman had arranged himself on a high cushion.

Cayman placed his hand on the box and spoke according to form. "Two days have you held this braid in contemplation. Do you wish to keep it?"

"I do," Jayan replied.

"Do you understand and accept that neither you nor your son, nor your son's descendants, will be allowed to shed in Shakti Lake?"

"Yes."

Cayman calculated the price as previously discussed, making sure to subtract the deposit Jayan had already put down for the braid. Jayan produced the correct sum in the form of a banknote prepared for him by Shakti-Patal Bank. His account there had grown on leftovers from his funded trips, royalties from the publication of his journals, and now his classes at Patal University and paid lectures at both universities.

Cayman accepted the orange banknote and gave Jayan a dated Shakti Lake Temple receipt, complete with Asta's name, her date of birth, the name of her Amala, and Cayman Natarajan's grandiose signature. Jayan set the rectangular card into notches on the underside of the fendelwood box lid.

"Congratulations," Cayman said with a chummy grip on Jayan's hand. The bursar couldn't be more pleased, as he had never expected a tongue-addled, virus-scarred destin to kindle such a bidding war. Gampoban-Saat had hung through it, and hadn't even disputed the extra fee for his mixed ethnicity. It was a fine sale indeed.

Cayman regarded Jayan for a moment, and then said with utmost politeness, "Will you be wearing that for your audience with Her Eminence Amala Tebbe?"

"Y—" Jayan started. He looked down at his bare chest and linen pants, and remembered his comfortably frayed sandals left behind in the foyer. "No?"

"I believe we can arrange for a more formal ensemble, if you are interested," Cayman said.

Jayan quirked his lips and nodded. He allowed Cayman's attendants to escort him to one of the private rooms.

One level below, in the stately foyer of Amala Tebbe's wing, Tebbe sat in a low chair positioned outside the closed sliding doors of her quarters. Selda, Tesame, and other acolytes stood near as Asta knelt at Tebbe's feet.

"Asta-la," Tebbe said. She stroked Asta's forehead and cheek. "You are always welcome here. Please visit us when you can."

Asta nodded. Vibrant thoughts of the bronze man—she had learned his name was Jayan—quelled any sadness she might have had over leaving the nursery. She would see Amala Tebbe again.

"Thank—thank—thank you," she said with more effort

than expected. She had been practicing the phrase. The other women murmured their approval.

An attendant signaled from the door. Tesame helped Asta stand up and then bent to smooth the skirt of her formal dress. They turned to stand beside Amala Tebbe, facing the main entrance, and with a final quick nudge at Asta to adjust her position, Tesame nodded to show they were ready.

Jayan Gampoban entered the foyer, every step accented with a tinkling from golden ankle bracelets spilling over his bare feet. He wore a wrapped skirt of deep green silk, with a matching white vest bordered in greens and gold. Cayman stood by the door as Jayan approached Amala Tebbe.

Asta's eyes followed Jayan with such a solid gaze that it took a fair amount of effort for him to tear his own eyes away from her. She wore a fitted gown embroidered with pink and white flowers—the cloth itself matched the deep green of Jayan's borrowed outfit. Cayman had planned it perfectly.

Jayan folded to both knees in front of Amala Tebbe, set the fendelwood box aside, and offered her the highest mudra of respect—pressed hands passing from forehead to throat to heart.

Tebbe met her own hands at her heart and bowed her head. "Jayan Gampoban. I am most pleased, and honored, to pass the braid of this destin, my daughter, to you."

"Thank you, Your Eminence." Jayan rose and turned to Asta while Tesame scooped Asta's elbows with open palms to let her know she may step forward. Asta met Jayan with outstretched hands, which he squeezed in his own.

"A destin no longer, Asta Gampoban is now your wife," Tebbe said.

Jayan grinned, and Asta blushed. She bowed her head as she had been coached, then felt his slightly chapped lips press her forehead. Hints of dried bark and fresh, dark soil met her nostrils.

She pondered this as Selda, Tez, and others descended with congratulatory hugs. She kept pondering as she and Jayan bowed with a farewell mudra for Tebbe, and as the two of them followed Cayman from the foyer . . . many things about this man were unexpected. His thick blue hair, for one. Her dreams had fashioned him completely bald, like a diver! Funny, considering that in real life his hands weren't even webbed.

Of course, a dream couldn't match the details of reality, where this man had chapped lips and matching rough-skinned fingertips. It was enough to see the pattern of gold scales at his wrists and ankles, against his brownish-bronze skin—the same features, remarkable and unmistakable, from the dreams where she'd already met him.

Asta stole a few glances at Jayan as they entered the main nursery building, and caught him stealing a few glances back. His hand—even if it was surprisingly coarse—had never let go of her own. He finally caught her eyes and smiled again with unabashed joy. That smile made it all fit. He knew of their connection as much as she did.

Cayman hurried forward to confer with two attendants at the main doors. The two slipped outside and clicked the doors shut as Cayman motioned for Asta and Jayan to wait. They could hear the distant hum of many combined voices, and then three tones from a gong just outside the door. The hum of voices ceased.

The attendants slid the doors open from the outside. With a guiding nudge from Cayman, Jayan and Asta preceded him onto the landing of the immense fanned staircase. Harsh sunlight cut Asta's eyes, so the only thing she could comprehend at first was Jayan's fist gripping her fingers.

Then, a rising gush of applause met her ears. She saw them at last—hundreds of eyes lifted toward herself and Jayan, above an undulating stratum of blurred hands. The audience stretched from the base of the staircase to the park beyond, where a festival seemed to be taking place—

"In your honor," Cayman said. He took her other hand and led them down the long staircase to a waiting group of Jayan's friends and colleagues gathered at the bottom.

Asta had never expected to meet so many people within her first few steps outside of the nursery. Amid the warm clasped hands—some fully webbed and some not—and the gracious smiles and congratulatory speeches, she dimly heard Jayan's voice say more than once, "Where is Najat?"

Najat stood in the busy park with Gavind Sandarapan. Among all the out-of-town crafters selling wares from the festival booths, Gavind's father, Aubik, was one of the most famous. The blind potter and his wife, Gavina, were nearly beside themselves with joy over this opportunity to see— or in Aubik's case, touch and hear—their boy.

"I don't believe we've ever traveled up from the Bend so fast," Gavina told them in the moments before Jayan emerged from the nursery. "Such short notice. But we wouldn't think of missing it!"

The Sandarapan booth teemed with customers, so after a few more words with his parents and a promise to meet them at Jayan's banquet that night, Gavind moved with Najat to get a better view of the nursery's double doors.

"Shouldn't you be up there by now?" Gavind asked.

"Not required. I'll see them tonight," Najat said. He stepped slightly away from Gavind and rooted himself in a prime position to watch the doors over everyone else's heads.

Gavind pointed toward the lane near the steps and said, "There's Vin!"

Najat looked and saw Vin and Ram standing in the crowd, with Palen nearby. Palen had a mouthful of fried honey cake from one of the blackrock vendors temporarily stationed along the lane.

Gavind pointed across Najat toward the Medical Arts building, where a fantastic white tent stood at the edge of the park. A long line of people waited outside. Najat and Gavind traded glances. They knew that Amala Vengar had set herself up inside the tent, to grant audiences to her throngs of admirers. She often came away from such events with baskets full of jewelry and other gifts.

Najat looked back to the nursery and saw Big Selda meet her husband near the bottom of the stairs. The gruff barge oarsman held Seldan on his shoulders, and even at that distance, Najat could tell that the boy had grown considerably in the last year.

The nursery gong sounded, causing the crowds around Najat to push forward. Najat remained still, every joint locked into place. He involuntarily shielded himself against Gavind and all else around him, caught by the instinctive desire to focus solely on the top of the nursery steps.

Jayan emerged from the doors wearing formal attire and holding the hand of his new wife. Najat strained to see the woman's features from that distance, but one of her hands obscured her face as she protected her eyes from the sun. The white walls and steps of the nursery set off her clinging, dark green gown. Cayman appeared and led her down the steps with Jayan attached.

Just as her face became visible, Najat felt Gavind grip his arm and heard him say, "Vin and Ram are closer. Think we can get there?"

The crowd at the bottom of the steps enveloped Asta and Jayan, blocking Najat's view. He nodded and moved on wooden legs to follow Gavind across the park to the lane near Vengar's wing of the nursery.

Najat felt a fleeting moment of guilty relief that the Mahasagi, Dechen, and Rajung were currently occupied at the bedside of a patient in Medical Arts, and Amala Tebbe was comfortably resting in her quarters. He didn't even notice how the crowd parted to let him through or how everyone lifted their hands in reverent mudras as he passed.

"Look who I brought!" said Gavind, as they reached Ram and the other divers. The divers greeted Najat with mudras and broad smiles. They had not seen him since the day of Asta's birth.

Ram slapped Gavind's shoulder and addressed Najat, "Did this one tell you his news? Senior diver!" Vin reached over to rub Gavind's head while Gavind ducked, looking sheepish.

Najat smiled, not really hearing Ram's words. He could not see Jayan or Asta from this spot. He heard one of the divers say, "They should let you through."

A few people in front of them turned at these words, and upon registering Najat's presence, began tugging at their neighbors' arms. The crowd folded apart to create an aisle for Najat, whom they recognized as the Kumasagi and someone who shared Jayan's blood. Najat stalled again, even as the crowd expected him to step forward. At the end of the aisle, still surrounded by well-wishers and with her back slightly turned, stood Asta, resplendent and voluptuous in her formal gown.

Jayan's arm could be seen on the other side of Asta, as they both stood angled away from Najat, talking with—or in Asta's case listening to—Jayan's colleagues.

Najat's heartbeat quickened. He could sense Asta's kana from where he stood, as clearly as he had ever sensed the Mahasagi or Amala Tebbe.

Asta moved a hand to her sternum and turned her head to look at Jayan, then looked back the other way, searching among the crowd with a puzzled expression. Najat broke into a sweat.

"Do you Feel it?" Gavind said at his shoulder.

Najat could not have been more startled by Gavind's choice of words. He clamped down, raising shield over shield in an attempt to break the connection with Asta. Suddenly he noticed that the other divers, including Gavind, were all looking back toward the nursery with open, intense faces.

Najat Felt it then, familiar and bittersweet. The Skyfish.

Shaktis were approaching the lake on the other side of the nursery.

Everyone leapt into motion around Najat. He saw Selda point in the direction of the lake and speak urgently to Asta and Jayan and her husband all at once. Selda's husband handed Seldan to an older boy from the Diver School, just as more Udaka trainees appeared out of the crowd to surround Najat and the divers. Some of them had to bolt down their last bites of honey cake.

"Feels like four of them," said Ram. The crowd murmured and then broke into cheers as the news spread. Selda hurried up the main steps to the nursery as her husband took a different route toward the dock. The line outside Amala Vengar's tent scattered as Vengar emerged with her attendants. Ram and the other divers stripped down to their loincloths and threw their clothing to the young trainees.

"We'll be at the banquet," Gavind called to Najat before diving into the lane after the others. They cut under the nursery steps with hardly a splash on their way to the diver complex.

Most of the diver school boys followed the divers on foot, but Najat managed to snag the arm of one who had no clothes to carry. The crowd swallowed Asta and Jayan from his sight again. Najat felt so flushed that he feared his hand must have seared the boy's skin.

"Please take these to the temple annex," he said, handing the boy his sandals and long blue skirt. "You can leave it all on the stairs." He dove into the lane without waiting for the boy's reaction.

The crisp water came as a blessed shock. Najat chopped

the lane in the opposite direction from the divers, past the library and toward the grand theater, swimming as far away as possible from the cheering crowds, the nursery, and Asta.

~ * ~ * ~ * ~

When Najat returned to the Mahasagi's annex after a long and numbing swim, he found Dechen waiting for him at the top of the stairs.

She handed him a towel and said, "The Mahasagi is still bedside for a patient at Medical Arts. Rajung is with him."

Najat applied the towel to his arms and torso with cautious, slow pats. "Did you need something here?"

"The Mahasagi must remain in his trance. I came to check on you."

"That's hardly necessary."

"Najat-la." Dechen hooked him with her gaze. "When you saw Asta today, you ran."

Najat applied the towel with more vigor, rubbing everywhere all at once. He thought he had adequately shielded himself from Tebhan. He strode into the common room, rubbing both sides of his head through the towel, trying to escape Dechen's words even as she followed him.

"You cannot avoid her, Najat. And you shouldn't have to! Look at what you've accomplished in the last year. Look at what *she* has accomplished. Amala Tebbe went through great effort to mend Asta's diksha." Dechen stepped closer as Najat's face disappeared into the towel. She stretched to reach his exposed ear and said, "Asta does not even *remember* that night."

Najat dumped the soggy towel into Dechen's arms. He

marched with tight lips to a closet near his private bath and pulled out more towels and a robe. Then he marched to his sleeping quarters and came back with a clean loincloth on top of the pile in his arms. Dechen preceded him into the bath and was already filling the oval tub with hot water from the blackrock tanks.

She kept talking while Najat separated the towels on a counter, hung his robe, and set up a bucket and soap near a low faucet in the far wall. "You are both whole again," she said over the gushing water. "Asta is now a woman with her own mind—far, *far* removed from the pashi destin in the Nakshidra Grotto. You *must* acknowledge her as she stands beside Jayan."

Jars of moisturizing oils banged to the countertop under Najat's hands. He fumbled with a shaving blade and mirror, finally setting out everything in a staggered row.

Dechen appeared at his side. Najat froze and pressed his splayed fingers into the counter until his webbing darkened against the tiles.

"You need to face her, for Jayan's sake. You need to respect her as his wife. Let the be-diksha be your own experience—a lesson for you, nothing more."

Najat turned on Dechen. "I need a *bath*," he said. He took her by the shoulders and herded her out the door. "I NEED A BATH!" He slid the bathing doors shut with such force that they almost jumped their tracks.

"I KNOW!" she shouted from the other side.

Steam billowed around Najat. He stomped over to the full tub and turned off the faucets. Then he yanked off his loincloth, hunched to a squat near the faucet in the wall, and used a cloth from the bucket of soapy water to scrub himself from scalp to toes. Several wrist and ankle scales snapped under the effort, drawing blood.

After a sizzling cold rinse, he submerged himself in the steaming tub and instantly felt the soothing effects of aromatic bath salts. Dechen must have slipped them into the water. Najat rested his chin at the surface and indulged in a very long soak, all the while studying Dechen's words over and over in his mind.

~ CHAPTER 12 ~

Maore Natarajan gestured toward the lake beyond the nursery and told Asta, "This new batch of destins is surely a good omen for your union with Gampo-Saat."

Asta smiled. The two women stood at the widened lane near the library, as Cayman and Jayan directed porters to load Asta's few belongings into a pedicart. It was late afternoon, and many people still lingered in the park. Most of the booths remained open, especially those offering food and drink.

Asta felt tired after standing all afternoon to receive the good wishes of so many strangers and new friends. The banquet still lay ahead, and even before that, Jayan wanted to show her the temple.

With another smile, Asta bent to pick up Maore and Cayman's son, who had been hovering at her legs. She could never be too tired to expend some attention on this little one. Mathin's slight frame felt nearly weightless on her hip as he gazed up at her with wide, examining eyes.

"Beautiful," Asta said.

"We'll be sure to bring him tonight," Maore said.

Asta grinned wider and nodded her approval, bouncing the equally grinning Mathin on her hip. The promise made it easier to relinquish the boy back to Maore when Jayan finished with the pedicart. Maore coached Mathin to wave goodbye to the new couple and then followed Cayman toward the booths in the park.

"The pedaler will deliver your things into the care of the university for now," Jayan said. "Are your drawings in there?"

Asta nodded. She had packed everything herself after making sure that all her drawings—especially the ones from the portfolio—had been returned.

"Let's walk to the temple. We can get a pedicab from there when we're done." Jayan took her elbow and directed her away from the lane. They crossed into a corner of the park where a narrow brick pathway broke the ground under overgrown ferns and flowering vines.

"Did anyone ever tell you about the Kumasagi?" Jayan asked over his shoulder as she walked behind him.

Asta had to lift the skirts of her gown away from reaching creeper vines as her formal slippers gathered dirt from the unswept path. She shook her head at his question. She had only heard of a *Maha*-sagi.

"The Kumasagi is like a younger version of the Mahasagi. He's thought to be a secondary incarnation of the same being. They share the same kana." Jayan glanced back. Asta was still fiddling with her skirts. "We're going to visit him."

Asta looked up. She hadn't known they would do more

than sightsee at the temple.

Jayan continued, "I don't understand it myself exactly, but they call it a double incarnation. When Mahasagi Tebhan dies, the Kumasagi will take his place as Mahasagi. I think he's supposed to absorb Tebhan's kana. It will be one entity for a while, but then the kana will split again, and a new Kumasagi will be found. Like a cycle of reincarnation," Jayan rotated his index fingers over each other, "but often there are two of them alive at the same time."

Asta found this confusing, but she was accustomed to figuring things out later after a bit of mulling. She wondered why they were going to meet the Kumasagi at all. Maybe Jayan didn't rate an audience with the Mahasagi himself? That hardly made sense, considering how the temple had thrown a whole festival in Jayan's honor.

Jayan did not take time to explain. When they reached the wider lane and could walk side by side again, she saw a half-hidden smirk on his face, as if there were more to the story but she would just have to wait. Asta shook out her skirts—slightly smudged on the bottom—over her soiled shoes and slipped her hand into Jayan's, enjoying his playful manner.

More congratulatory strangers surrounded them on the noisy rear deck of the temple. Active little boys, cheerful adults, and unhurried elder folks spilled from the mouth of the temple's merchant corridor, where numerous kiosks and blackrock vendors supplemented the main temple shops during the festival.

Asta looked up. The sprawling, balconied tiers of Shakti Lake Temple looked much more impressive towering over her head than they had from her previous view through the nursery windows across the park. The talking faces in front of her, the aroma of cooked foods, and the colorful clothes all around them served to excite her and somehow also drain her.

Jayan said by her ear, "You can see more if we go this way." He bowed through more well-wishers and pulled her by the hand into the merchant corridor. The polished wood ceiling and floors amplified the noise of the crowds. "But we don't really have time to stop," he yelled over his shoulder.

Asta's tired legs protested as Jayan led her up a flight of stairs to the second floor, but her ears found relief in the diminishing sounds of the crowd. Jayan walked by her side again and said, "This is the back way . . . or the front way, depending on how you view it." They encountered two temple attendants who bowed, smiled, offered mudras, and let them pass.

"I'm not even sure if he's here," Jayan whispered as they crossed an elevated, enclosed walkway with dark wooden floors and faded woven rugs. Asta looked through the windows and saw the water lane pass directly beneath them.

They reached the Mahasagi's annex on the other side, where a wide landing opened out over a switchback staircase. Jayan pointed down the steps and said, "That's how I usually come up."

Asta removed her slippers as Jayan removed his sandals and the gold ankle bracelets borrowed from Cayman. Asta questioned him with her eyes but he just handed it all to her with a toss of his hand, as if he never cared to wear a speck of gold again.

She tucked the bracelets into her slippers and put their shoes on a low shelf while Jayan peered through a crack in the doorway to their left. "Someone must be here if they left this open," he said. He slid the door open further and led Asta into a long and silent room.

It seemed to be a waiting area. Jayan motioned for Asta to sit, and she did so with much relief on a low cushioned bench near the windows, where the temple balconies were visible across the lane. Sliding screens made of wood and paper stood closed at the far end of the room. Jayan walked to the nearer, long side of the room and knocked on a smaller door, which Asta almost missed at first because it was made of the same dark wood as the walls.

Someone opened the door to an eye's width.

"Ai," said Jayan.

The door opened further, just enough to let Jayan slip inside. Asta obeyed another wave from Jayan's hand and stayed behind as the door closed.

She settled back on the cushions and rested her tired legs. She could hear Jayan's voice, muffled and unintelligible on the other side of the door. A deep bass voice answered Jayan's pauses, but she could not decipher the speaker's words.

Asta gazed at a small table nearby, where a teapot sat next to stacks of upside down cups and right side up saucers. She reached over and felt the side of the teapot. It was cold. She lifted the lid and peered inside. It was empty.

Jayan emerged from the door and closed it behind him. "Asta," he said.

She stood up, feeling a rush of pleasure at the sound of her name from his lips. Jayan led her to the formal, paper-screened doors at the end of the room, slid them open, and ushered her inside.

This room was more spacious. Large windows spanned the wall across from them and also the wall to their right, reminding Asta of her favorite corner nook at the nursery. Tall potted plants softened the light into dappled shadows below the windows.

A door slid open on the left, and the Kumasagi stepped into the room. He walked directly to the couple and tilted his head with a welcoming smile for Asta, hands pressed together at his sternum.

Asta looked up at this man, tall and bronzed, with golden scales and luminous brown eyes and a head shaved bare as a diver's, and felt her mind suddenly empty, suddenly falling and crashing, shattering loudly in her head to a thousand pieces at her feet.

She recognized him immediately—not from the Nakshidra Grotto, which she truly did not remember, but from her clear and cherished dream of him above the burial lake.

"Najat, this is Asta," Jayan said. "Asta, this is His Eminence the Kumasagi. Najat *Gampoban*."

Asta slid her eyes to Jayan as the surname knocked against her wooden brain. *This* was the joke. This was the joke that Jayan Gampoban—a sudden stranger to her now—had hidden in a smirk and now blatantly trumpeted from the broadening grin on his face. She looked back at Najat, trying to process the physical similarities between the two men.

Najat maintained his patient smile.

"My ama bore a second child," Jayan said. He laughed

and wiggled Asta's shoulder under his hand, as if to shake away her disbelief. "Najat and I have the same parents."

Najat tipped his head again and said, "I am the younger." Asta felt his sonorous voice reverberate off her bones, and remembered the gray water sliding through her legs and the soft, unseen sand sucking at her heels. Her face tingled from a sudden lack of blood.

Najat stepped back, and a ray of late afternoon light caught the silver torc at his neck. Even his blue skirt matched that in the dream, but now his shoulders and arms were concealed by a loose silk jacket of the same dark color. He motioned to several cushions on the floor near a low platform. "Please sit. Would you like tea?"

"No, we can't stay long," Jayan said. He dropped onto a cushion. "I still want to show Asta the apartment before the banquet."

Asta stumbled a little on the cushions, gathered up the skirts of her gown, and sat down a few steps away from Jayan. The walls settled around her, and she inwardly thanked herself for not fainting.

Najat stepped onto the platform and folded into an elegant half-lotus pose on top of a thin, ornately embroidered cushion. A taller, wider, and even more ornate cushion occupied the center of the platform just next to Najat. "His Eminence the Mahasagi is not here at the moment," Najat said, "but I'm sure he would have liked to greet you."

"That's alright. We only stopped by to see you," Jayan said.

Asta twisted her skirts in her hands. She could not comprehend it. Jayan had said the Mahasagi and Kumasagi

173

were like a double incarnation of the same person. But she was seeing double now with just Jayan and Najat in the room.

She could see Najat's sternum and a hint of ribs where his jacket lay open. He was thinner than Jayan, and just a touch taller. Najat looked at her and said in a voice aged well beyond his appearance, "Is this your first visit to the temple?"

Small talk? Asta could only stare at him with slightly gapped lips. It was the same type of conversation that various folks from the festival had offered her. *Najat.* She practiced his name in her mind, hoping for some greater connection. This apparition from her dream appeared to have no remembrance of her.

Jayan's voice startled her. "Asta is still learning to speak, so she's a little shy. But she'll start speech therapy soon at Medical Arts."

Asta turned her stare on Jayan. It was the first time she had heard of this.

Jayan continued talking to Najat, "I don't know why the nursery didn't have someone look at her sooner. I set up the appointments myself right after I bought the braid."

Najat smiled and said to Asta, "I'm sure they will take good care of you there."

Asta's teeth dented her lower lip. She had no response for this. Jayan said something beside her, but she forgot to listen. Najat still looked at her, even as Jayan talked, and she noticed how Najat's full mouth and broad nose were similar to Jayan's. She noticed how Najat's eyes were larger and wider set. She watched as those eyes narrowed slightly, the lower lids crinkling and almost seeming to twitch. Asta Felt a jolt in the center of her chest.

Najat tipped his head slowly, almost imperceptibly, as Asta Felt her ribs expand. Then he turned back to Jayan and nodded in the pauses of Jayan's self-maintained conversation. Asta could not possibly listen to Jayan herself. Najat's warmth radiated inside her, where the jolt had anchored an open line between them. The line transmitted so much more than what showed on his face. She Felt his curiosity, and saw his eyes glance back to check her response.

Her newfound real-world instinct—and the hint of caution that she Felt through the line—told her to sit still even as she wanted to leap toward him and shout, *It's you!* Now she understood that he had wondered if *she* recognized *him*. She bled her sentiments through the line to him, not at all practiced at it but sure he would catch the confirmation.

Najat's face showed no change, but Asta could Feel his grateful response. A voice addressed her from the left.

Jayan. Asta looked at him, startled again. "You will, won't you?" Jayan asked with a smile.

Asta nodded, having no idea what he spoke of.

"Asta? Are you okay?" Jayan moved to a cushion beside her.

She felt tears in her eyes and flushed, suddenly panicked by the idea that she might panic. Her breath caught as Najat severed the connection from his end. Asta quickly dabbed her eyes but then immediately wished that she hadn't tried to dab—it only encouraged Jayan's concern. He gripped her shoulder.

"Perhaps she is tired?" Najat said from the platform.

"Ah, is that it?" Jayan weaved his head, trying to meet Asta's eye. She nodded without looking up. He rubbed his palm up and down her shoulder. "We still have a banquet to attend. Think you can get through it?"

She nodded again.

Najat stood and walked to them as Jayan helped Asta up. "Well, I'm glad we could meet you alone," Jayan said to Najat. "But you'll be there tonight?"

"Yes, of course," Najat said.

Asta looked up at Najat, all tears absorbed before falling. He nodded to her and smiled with the same politeness everyone else had shown her that day. The air between them felt purposefully empty, as if something that should be there had been removed.

She turned away from his meaningless smile and followed Jayan out.

"Let's find a cab," Jayan said. Asta followed him down the staircase, carrying the gold ankle bracelets for him. Jayan, the man who had bought her braid and now called her his wife, said over his shoulder, "I forgot to tell you . . . you're supposed to offer the highest mudra to the Kumasagi when you greet him."

Asta gazed at Jayan's unfamiliar back. She knew he expected no answer.

Two floors above them, in the silent waiting area with dark wooden walls, Najat's shaking legs could no longer hold him. He dropped onto the bench near the empty teapot and remained there until dusk fell outside and all light drained from the room.

~ * ~ * ~ * ~

Asta remembered little from the banquet at Patal University, other than watching Najat from afar as he talked and ate with the weary, yet jubilant divers. He did not accompany the divers when they approached the head table in small groups to pay their respects to Jayan's new wife.

Jayan sat to Asta's left, his attention commanded by the stories of an old friend of Cayman's named Padir, who had just returned from an excursion to the Kandargiri cliffs by the Southern Sea. Jayan leaned over once or twice and offered an excuse to guests who tried to converse with Asta, "She'll start speech therapy soon." Asta kept her mouth shut.

She did enjoy more time with little Mathin, as Maore sat near her and shared the toddler generously. Padir had brought his shy son, Sopan, whom Mathin stared at throughout the meal with burgeoning admiration—Sopan being the elder by two years. Mathin, a pure-born son of Shakti Lake with gray skin, silver scales, and white hair, was fascinated by Sopan's light green skin and straight, ink-black hair. Sopan's mother—absent from the festivities—was a daughter of Kandargiri.

Sopan warmed up, and even smiled, after Asta charmed him with a game of wrestling thumbs. By the end of the evening, the boys and Asta had formed a solid camaraderie, with Sopan talking the most, Mathin repeating half of what he said, and Asta left with little else but the giggles.

The boys distracted Asta from watching Najat, and his place sat long empty by the time Maore retrieved Mathin and said goodnight. The divers had left earlier than most, quite exhausted from the harvest that afternoon, which had yielded six destins. Selda and Tesame had been invited to the banquet as well, but they remained at the nursery to help watch over the pashi destins until the Amalas could perform diksha.

A few days earlier, Tesame had coached Asta on what would happen after the wedding banquet. Asta thought of this as she walked with Jayan back up to his—and now their—apartment, located two terraces above the main university hall. When they arrived, he apologized again for the mess. She had already seen it on their first short visit to the apartment before the banquet.

"I'm still trying to organize things," he said.

"I could—I could—I could help," Asta said.

Jayan held up a glass jar with a neat, handwritten label. "How's your reading and writing?"

She lowered her eyes. "Not good."

"We'll have to get that fixed, too." He led her into the bedroom. "But we don't need to worry about it right at the moment."

Asta knew what occupied Jayan's mind right at the moment. She unpacked a jar of fancy spiced oil as Jayan lit a few candles near the head of the wide bedroll. The oil had been a parting gift from the nursery—a bit of tradition for the new wife's first night. Jayan seemed to know about the tradition as well. He removed his silk jacket and wrapped skirt, and lay on the bed in only his loincloth, watching Asta.

She knelt over the bed and started on Jayan's right arm. Tesame's instructions had been verbal, of course, so this was Asta's first hands-on experience with touching a man. As she massaged his upper arm, she noticed a few crackly patches along Jayan's skin, and wondered if he used enough tari oil each day.

His arm flinched as her fingers moved below his elbow. There was a long scar on the underside, running diagonally from his elbow crease to the gold scales at his wrist. It was a fresh, puckered scar, scarcely healed, and tender to the touch. Asta decided to avoid it. She gave special attention to massaging his webless hand instead.

She massaged his shoulders and left arm and hand, and then moved down to his feet to rub the oil from his toes to his calves, and over his knees to his upper thighs. He verbalized his pleasure with low grunts and an occasional rumbling moan. Asta tried her best to push away thoughts of Najat Gampoban's voice, so rich and deep.

After she massaged Jayan's back, he rested for a moment, and then turned to his side and took the oil from her. He reached over to where she knelt and untied the straps of her gown. The cloth fell to a puddle at her waist, leaving her torso exposed.

He smiled and held her gaze with his brown eyes—so similar to Najat's—and caught one of her hands in his own. His other hand lifted toward her, so similar to the tender, bronze hand that had reached toward her at the burial lake. Asta leaned closer, expecting a caress at her cheek.

Jayan's fingers met her left breast. The rest of his hand followed, denting her flesh. This sudden return to reality startled Asta so thoroughly that she failed to catch her breath before Jayan's mouth covered hers. His lips felt as chapped as his hands. His tongue tasted dry in her mouth.

179

Asta decided that this might be the wrong time to daydream about ancient burial lakes and deep mystical connections. Jayan lifted her so that the rest of her gown slid off, and pulled her onto the bed. She let her mind go blank, save for the memory of Tesame's stolid voice instructing her on what comes next after the spiced oil massage.

~ CHAPTER 13 ~

No one was surprised when Jayan left Shakti Lake City within a tenday of buying his wife. Even Asta knew him well enough by then, and she halfway expected it to happen.

At the wedding banquet, Padir Dagarapan had mesmerized Jayan with stories of his expeditions. Jayan met with Padir several times over the days that followed. Padir had recently traveled south to observe the giant birds called lopperbeaks that nested in the Kandargiri cliffs, near the mouth of the Nagi River.

"Amala Tangar's destin pool is inside a cave in the shorter cliff," Jayan told Asta. "That area is infested with lopperbeaks. They're dangerous—they've attacked and killed people. The Kandargirians have been battling them for generations. Amala Vengar was born there. Padir's wife, too."

Padir Dagarapan lived under a cliff himself, part way up Dagaragiri Mountain on the eastern edge of Patal Valley. He had long been obsessed with the Kandargiri lopperbeak, and he had long held the desire to somehow tame one of the birds.

"He hasn't figured out how to do it, in all the years he's studied the lopperbeaks. But now someone has emerged who can mind meld with the birds, and control them. A young mystic in Kandargiri. Padir knows him."

"Do birds even have minds?" Asta said.

Jayan laughed. He didn't care how it worked. He just wanted to see it for himself. He had lucked into meeting Padir through Cayman Natarajan at the wedding banquet. Padir and his crew, including his four-year-old son Sopan, were on a supply run in Shakti Lake City before heading back south to visit Kandargiri again. They had no trouble convincing Jayan to go with them.

"Padir and Cayman used to be business partners," Jayan told Asta. "They owned the blackrock mines on the other side of Dagaragiri. Now Padir owns the whole thing, but he lets his managers run it for him. He easily funds his own trips to study the lopperbeaks."

Jayan promised to take Asta on another adventure sometime. He had little experience with the lopperbeaks or the Kandargiri cliffs, as he always chose to detour around them when traveling to his birthplace on Sindhupat Island. An adult lopperbeak could be the size of a two-story house.

Asta could have protested that whatever adventure a four-year-old was welcome to, a woman should also be welcome to. But she had little interest in joining the expedition, and chose not to argue.

The only problem left for Jayan was how to delicately abandon his third-quarter classes at the university, which were due to start the same day Padir planned to push off at the Nagi River. With some quick thinking and several desperate meetings—though he in no way let himself appear desperate—Jayan managed to convince the university deans to combine his two seminar classes into one field class, where the students were invited to accompany the expedition.

Perhaps Cayman helped a little with some gifts and promised favors to the geography department, but Jayan pretended not to know. The university then had to appease the parents of the students whose classes had been upended. For most parents, the possible dangers of the expedition outweighed the prestige of traveling with Jayan Gampoban. There were some takers, but then Jayan had the even more rigorous task of convincing Padir to let any one of them come along.

Between the irked parents and the grumbling Padir, Jayan eked out four students to join the expedition. Padir made sure that each of them was either athletic in build or just plain strong, all the better to help carry provisions and paddle the canoes.

The day before Jayan left, he took Asta on his traditional walk around the edge of Shakti-Patal Plateau. Najat declined an invitation to join them, as Tebhan was attending the death of an aged Lake Kalan acolyte and wanted Najat by his side.

Jayan and Asta started out early and stopped at Eastview Teahouse. Suchal—one year taller and still just as lanky—served them breakfast with silent admiration. His mother yelled at him only twice during the course of Jayan and Asta's meal.

After leaving the teahouse, Jayan and Asta walked along

the wall to the northern edge of the plateau, which took the better part of the morning. Jayan grinned at Asta's wide-eyed reaction to the incredible views of the eastern valley, and grinned even wider at her reaction when they reached the north edge near Utaragiri Mountain.

They entered another teahouse, called the Waterview, which had a much larger deck than the Eastview. While they waited for lunch, they stood at the deck's rail to look over the northern edge of the plateau.

A deep crevasse separated the back of the plateau from the towering, steep mountain of Utaragiri. The Nagi River came crashing down Utaragiri Falls, located diagonally across the crevasse from where Jayan and Asta stood. Aqueducts beamed out from the falls to divert some of the Nagi directly over the crevasse, into the industrial waterworks at the back of the plateau.

The remainder of the Nagi fell into the crevasse. Most of it flowed west to more aqueducts and piping systems and the Patal Valley riverbed. Some of it trickled east, through the crevasse below the Waterview Teahouse and around the side of the plateau, to become the Thin River.

Asta could see the buildings of a vacation resort nestled among flowering green ledges near the great waterfall. A large portion of the mountain face across from the Waterview had been carved into terraced fields by the generations of farmers and fisher folk who lived there. Looking down, she could see a fishery spanning both sides of the river inside the crevasse.

Jayan raised his voice over the roar of the waterfall and asked her, "Do you know the geography of the valley?"

She raised one hand and tilted it to indicate she

knew a little.

He pulled a journal from his pack and opened it to a blank page, then pulled out a pencil and handed everything to her. "Show me what you know."

They walked back to their cushions. Asta sat down and began to draw. She drew a large wavy circle in the middle of the page. "Mountains," she said, indicating the edge of the circle. She gestured inside the circle without drawing. "Patal— Patal—Patal Valley."

Jayan nodded.

Asta drew a small square inside the circle, near the top. She gestured at the square, "Shakti— Shakti—Shakti-Patal Plateau." She drew a small oval inside the square to indicate the destin lake. "Shakti Lake City."

Jayan nodded again. "Where's the river?"

Asta glanced up at the waterfall beyond the deck's rail and bent to draw again. She squiggled some lines just above the square that represented the plateau. That was the waterfall. Then she drew a long, thick line straight down from the waterfall, hooking it around the left side of the plateau, then all the way down through the center of the valley. "Nagi River," she said.

Jayan kept nodding. "Anything else?"

She indicated the right side of the plateau. "Another river?"

He took the sketchbook and pencil from her and added his own markings to her map. "Right, the Nagi splits at the plateau." He drew a thin double line from the waterfall around the right side of Shakti-Patal Plateau. "Thin River. You saw it from the last teahouse, and when we walked the eastern wall to get here. You can also see it from Patal

University."

Asta nodded.

Jayan shaded a kinked area of the river, just south of the plateau. "There is a town here called Thin River Bend. Their market is famous. All the best crafters live down here." From that point he hooked the river sharply to the right and scribbled a blob near the foot of Dagaragiri Mountain. "That is Patalaiya Lake. Lots of good fishing there, and boating—and swimming, of course."

He moved back to her rendering of the larger Nagi River and gestured over it, just south of the plateau. "The lower destin lakes are here."

Asta looked up at him, surprised.

"You didn't know?" He regarded her for a moment. "The instructors in the nursery taught you about the destin pools and lakes, right? Can you name all the current Amalas?"

Asta shook her head.

"Didn't they—? What have you been doing for the past year?"

"I—I—I—" *I've been—*

She was embarrassed. There were too many things that she didn't know. She loved Selda and Tesame and Amala Tebbe, but now she regretted how they had let her be alone, off by herself with her sketchbooks and pencils, while the other destins went through a more formalized instruction that included reading and writing, with some history, basic geography, and math.

They had tried to cram it in during her twenty-day grooming schedule after Vengar forced her to the block, but she had been too upset at the time to pay attention to the lessons.

Even up to the moment when she stepped on the block, she hadn't known that the people of the world came in many shades, not just silver and gray. Somehow she missed the cue of Amala Vengar's green skin and black hair.

She wondered if other destins came off the block that daft.

Jayan went on about the destin lakes of the valley. "Three of them are still active. The temple administration calls them the 'Lesser Lakes,' but you'll hear people refer to them as the 'Lower Lakes.' One of them is really big, but the other two are smaller. Lake Agra, Lake Kalan, and Lake Khurd." He added three circles arranged in a vertical line to indicate the lakes, then laughed. "They do things a little differently down there."

A serving boy brought their food then, but Jayan wasn't finished with the map. He held the sketchbook on his knee and kept drawing.

Across the page, below the lower corner of Patal Valley, he drew a large blobby shape near the Southeastern Sea. "That's the Old City of Ayunath. It's kind of far from Shakti Lake City, but there's a passage through the mountains there for people who want to visit the southeast beaches."

He pointed to where the end of the Nagi River met the end of the valley. "The Nagi River flows through a gorge here called Ora Canyon, and ends up at the Southern Sea. Here's Kandargiri Cliff and Achilagiri Cliff." He tapped the cliffs with his pencil. "The lopperbeaks nest all through here."

He remembered something. "And there is a giant wood-and-stone wall right here," he drew a line across Ora Canyon, part way up from the sea, "Bachanagoda Gate—or

Bachan Gate. It was built to stop the lopperbeaks from roaming further up the canyon."

Asta scratched her chin and watched him. Jayan seemed lost in thought, gazing down at the map.

"I've been everywhere on this map," he said. "And so many places not on this map. But I've never spent more than half a day at Kandargiri."

She could tell by his intense, lip-bitten expression that he couldn't wait to get down to those cliffs. He looked up and saw her watching him.

"Oh!" Jayan waved his pencil. "Don't worry about us—about me. Padir has been to Kandargiri more times than I can count on both hands."

Asta remembered one more thing for the map. "Where is your island?"

Jayan drew another mountain across a valley to the west from Kandargiri. "Well, this is Nichagiri." He gestured his pencil beyond Nichagiri, over the wavy lines he had drawn for the ocean. "Sindhupat Island is further this way. Off the page." He smiled. "I'll definitely take you to Sindhupat. Najat and I grew up there—until he was nine years old, when he left with the Mahasagi. I left when I was fifteen."

Asta knew that Najat and Jayan had grown up there. She bent to her food and started eating.

~ * ~ * ~ * ~

Before sunrise the next morning, Jayan stuffed the journal with Asta's map into his travel pack, then headed out from their apartment after a long, crushing hug and chapped kiss for Asta. He would meet Padir and the rest of their traveling party at the banks of the Greater Nagi on the opposite side of the plateau, where Padir owned a dock full of river canoes.

He couldn't tell Asta exactly how many tendays the trip would take. "I'll send a flier to let you know when we're heading back to Shakti Lake City."

She noticed that he called it "Shakti Lake City" instead of "home."

It was still dark outside after Jayan left, so Asta went back to bed. She suddenly wondered what she would do for the next few tendays—she hadn't even thought to ask Jayan. He had only left her with instructions to leave everything that was his as it was—he would resume organizing the apartment when he returned. The only definite thing on her schedule was speech therapy, which she attended every other day in a clinic near Shakti Lake Medical Arts, back up on the plateau.

She fell asleep wondering about Najat, whom neither she nor Jayan had seen since the day of their marriage.

"You could volunteer at Medical Arts!" Maore told Asta.

Asta looked up from a bench in Maore's garden. She had Mathin on one knee and her sketchbook on the other, with Mathin studiously drawing shaky ovals and long arcs with her blunt pencil. Two ovals made a pair of eyes, and the arc a mouth, repeated over and over again across the page.

"Volunteer?" Asta said.

"Yes! On the children's floor. You could draw for the boys, or show them how to draw. You are so good with

Mathin. You like children, right?"

Asta nodded. Little boys were still new to her, as were many things outside of the nursery. But she felt at ease with Mathin, and pleasantly amused by him, and instinctively protective of him. She secretly looked forward to having a child of her own.

Maore took her to meet the doctors of the children's floor, who talked with her, and let her peek in on some patients, and warmly invited her to become a volunteer. Suddenly Asta found that she *would* have something worthwhile to occupy her time while Jayan was on his trip.

~ * ~ * ~ * ~

Although Jayan taught courses in geography, his real boss at Patal University was Purnima Janipan, Dean of the Department of Botany and Horticulture. She had recommended and championed Jayan to the geography department, and served as his guarantor during his first year as a guest professor.

Dean Jani, as her colleagues and students entitled her, had hoped Jayan could eventually join her own department. But his lack of formal schooling on any subject, and thus his lack of certifications, made it impossible to give him a professorship—it had been difficult enough to gain him the title of guest professor, which he rated by way of practical experience and celebrity, rather than credentials.

And now his lack of discipline put even that adjunct position in jeopardy, as he proved to be a poor and infrequent communicator during his travels with

Padir Dagarapan.

Five days after Padir's expedition began, Dean Jani sent a message runner to summon Jayan's wife.

Asta had only just arrived home from Shakti Lake City when the messenger came to her door with Dean Jani's note. When Asta admitted that she didn't know the way, he offered to lead her through the cascading, jumbled campus of the university below.

There were high, grassy overlooks to traverse, bordered by sturdy safety rails, and low, shadowed courtyards paved all around in stone. Stairways, swim lanes, and herringbone brick paths flowed as directed by blue-lettered signage and the occasional placarded map.

Several terraces down, a long, domed wall of sectioned glass enclosed the university's grand botanical gardens. The end of it was not glass, but a solid, multistoried attachment of classrooms and laboratories.

As instructed by the message runner, Asta climbed several flights of stairs to a foyer at the top of the building. A friendly receptionist escorted her to the dean's office.

The office was wide, with walls painted a lovely pale green. A long, gently arched window revealed a view of the gardens below. Precisely organized bookcases framed the window on either side, while Dean Jani's desk stood in front, perfectly centered below the apex of the window.

The dean's two assistants sat at smaller desks on either side of the room, stealing glances at Asta while they worked. Asta paused on an invisible mark between the distant side desks, halfway between the office door behind her and the garden window in front. Most visitors found themselves drawn to that very spot in the center of the room.

Dean Jani sat on the cushions behind her low desk. She was a tall woman, with the strong and lithe body of a swimmer. Her short white hair and pure white scales stood out from her dark gray skin—rare attributes for one born of a lower valley lake.

She noticed Asta's tunic with the pale green collar. "Shakti Lake Medical Arts?" Dean Jani said.

"Yes, I'm just a—just a—just—just a volunteer. Today was my—my—my first—"

"What have you heard from Jayan about his trip?"

Asta hesitated. "Nothing yet."

"He has sent you nothing? In five days? No letters?"

Asta noticed an open flier packet in the dean's webbed hand. "Is that—is that from him?" Asta asked.

"Yes, but it's only a sentence. No *details*. He only said they've finished the first portage of the Nagi, where it starts to bend. I thought you would have a letter from your husband by now."

"He said he would send me a message when they—when they—when they start back from—from Kandargiri."

Dean Jani uttered a strong word under her breath. "Never mind, then. You may go."

She barely noticed Asta's retreat as she stared down at the short message from Jayan.

"He didn't even mention his students," Dean Jani said to her main assistant. Her assistant looked up, but saw that she didn't require a response. He returned to grading exams.

Three days later, Asta surprised them by visiting Dean Jani's office without an appointment.

Dean Jani set aside a large map she had been reading, focused her attention on Jayan's wife, and asked, "Have you received any news from Jayan?"

"No . . . ah, I—I—I thought maybe you have."

"Oh, we *have*." Dean Jani pulled a flier note from a stack of papers. She held it up so that Asta could see how much blank space surrounded Jayan's scribbled words. Then she tossed it aside. "They've left the last camp of the valley. Their next stop is Orasarana. He gave no more details than that."

The dean returned to looking at her map, which outlined the site of her latest pet project, a new aquatic garden to be designed and built by her students.

Asta stood there, her eyes caught by a framed drawing on the middle shelf of Dean Jani's bookcase. It was a water lily in bloom, drawn in green and black inks by Asta's own hand. Jayan must have given it to Dean Jani without Asta knowing.

Dean Jani's main assistant cleared his throat.

"Is there anything else?" Dean Jani said to Asta without looking up.

"No, Saati," Asta said. "Thank you, Saati." Asta exchanged a quick mudra with the dean's assistant on her way out.

Dean Jani grumbled over her map. "He doesn't even write to his own wife . . ." She couldn't fathom why a man like Jayan would buy himself a braid in the first place.

~ CHAPTER 14 ~

Asta didn't care to have any further visits with Dean Janipan. She spent her mornings in the grand library at the temple complex, poring over picture books with simple words in an effort to develop her reading and writing skills, such as they were.

She also attended her speech therapy sessions, and enjoyed walking to the public pier of red Shakti Lake. She gave little thought to exploring the campus of Patal University or the terraced villages on that side of the plateau. She preferred to return to Shakti Lake City, even if it required a vigorous hike up the southeastern stairpath each day.

Maore Natarajan insisted that Asta stay in her home as often as she liked. Little Mathin called her Auntie Asta but treated her as his number one playmate, and threw a fit whenever it was time for her to go.

Asta also spent some evenings in the nursery, visiting with Tesame.

She felt shy when volunteering at Medical Arts until she discovered how easy it was to amuse the young patients. She drew simple cartoon stories, often by their suggestions, or helped the boys draw pictures of their own.

When she needed a respite from Medical Arts, she often took her sketchbook into the temple park to work on her nature studies. Everyone kept telling her she would need that skill the most.

One day while she was sitting in the park, Najat Gampoban strolled up the path and sat down on the bench beside her.

Asta's heart skipped when she saw him walk toward her, and she had to take a sly, slow breath to calm herself. Najat exuded the same casual, tediously polite manner that he had when they parted the last time. She decided to use the same approach.

He tipped his head to her and bowed from his shoulders before taking the seat. Asta tipped her own head and offered him a dignified, ceremonial mudra. Her pencil caught in the pale webbing between her fingers.

She snatched the pencil to her lap as Najat said in his great rumbling voice, "Hello."

She tipped her head again. "Hello."

Najat's face tightened, for just a sliver of a second, and his lips mashed together, as if some expression strained underneath but he didn't want to reveal it. Asta realized that she had just spoken aloud to him for the first time.

He quickly relaxed his face to hide his reaction, and chose an obvious question. "Have you heard from Jayan?"

She almost shook her head, but then she corrected herself. Padir Dagarapan had sent a flier to the Natarajans,

195

and Jayan had sent his fliers of few words to Patal University, and so she had learned of their travel updates.

"They made—made—made it to the canal leading to—to—to Orasarana. Probably further by now."

"How are you?" Najat asked.

"Busy!" Asta smiled.

"Oh—" Najat braced his hands on his knees, as if to get up.

"Ai! Not busy now," Asta said. She indicated her sketchbook and the park around them. "Taking a—taking a—a—a break."

"Ah." Najat's eyes crinkled and he relaxed again. "I heard that you've made an impression over at Medical Arts."

She blushed and fiddled with her pencil.

"Jayan will be pleased."

Asta's fingers stopped fiddling. She looked back up at Najat. "What are you doing today?"

"The Mahasagi is with a patient. His First and Second Hands are there, too." Najat stretched out his long legs. "Sometimes I go with them, to observe him and learn. If I don't go with them, I'm supposed to stay up there," he pointed toward the Mahasagi's annex jutting out from the temple, "and meditate. But sometimes I go for a walk or a swim instead."

She raised her eyebrows at him and his cheeks dented in response. "I can meditate just as easily when walking or swimming as I can with my ass sitting on the floor," he said.

Asta burst out laughing.

Najat paused. He hadn't meant to make her laugh. He continued as if the sweet sound of it didn't affect him. "I felt . . . restless today. Like I needed to be outside."

Asta watched him as he looked off toward the library, then back to the other side of the park. He glanced at her with a taut expression.

Asta smiled, trying to stay relaxed. She lifted her sketchbook and tilted it toward him.

"May I see?" he asked, and slid to her side of the bench.

She opened the sketchbook to a different page than he expected. She pointed to the colorful dashed lines and vigorous looping squiggles on the page.

"Mathin Natarajan," she said.

"Ah, Cayman's boy." Najat used his thumb to press back the crinkled edges of the paper, where Mathin's enthusiasm had left as many wrinkles as crayon marks.

Asta nodded. "And some—some—some boys from Medical Arts. The sick—the sick ones." She turned the pages and showed him more scribbles, and a few decent attempts at lizards and birds by the older boys. After a bit of prodding from Najat, she even showed him her own recent sketches . . . anything to prolong this moment, with his shoulder almost brushing her cheek and his breath warming her brow.

Asta reached out an unspoken tendril of Feeling, much more cautious than the emotional overflow of their first meeting. She discovered a wall—a thin, crystalline barrier that seemed to hover an inch off Najat's skin, transparent to her eyes but not her inner senses. Najat cleared his throat and turned another page of the sketchbook. Asta tapped gently against the ice-hard glaze. She could sense his kana beneath it, dense and warm and sparkling, but she could not Touch through.

A sudden pressure seized Asta by the ribs. It was not

from Najat. They both heard a distant voice cry out.

Asta's breath caught as she rose from the bench, clutching the front of her tunic where the pain seared into her lungs. The sketchbook slid from her knees and bounced across the path.

Najat stood up beside her, alarmed.

She still couldn't breathe, the pain cut her so deeply. She felt Najat's long fingers wrap her shoulders. "Look at me," he said. "*Look!*"

The shock doubled her over, making it impossible to look up. Tears dropped directly out of her eyes to the mosaic path below.

"Look at my feet," he said. "Just look at my feet."

She looked at his feet, and felt clarifying energy spider out from his fingers, permeating the muscles across her shoulders and back. Najat's long, webbed toes pressed into the small gray and white tiles of the path. She realized for the first time that his feet were bare. He wore the kind of ankle cuffs that Jayan hated, except these were silver instead of gold.

She lifted her hands to the cool scales at his wrists. The scorching pain in her chest dulled to a lazy throb as they both heard a dim voice cry out again from behind the library, "*Call for doctors! Boys School! Emergency!*"

Asta finally looked up at Najat. He turned back from gazing in the direction of the voice and searched Asta's eyes, squeezing her soft shoulders. "You Felt it before I did," he said.

Someone else yelled from a corner of the park near the library, "Call for doctors!"

They needed more voices to relay the message. Najat

swung Asta to the side without letting her go and shouted toward the Medical Arts building, "CALL FOR DOCTORS! TO THE BOYS SCHOOL!"

Asta's bones rattled from the force of his booming voice. Several heads appeared on the balconies of the temple. "Call for doctors!" they yelled. More voices picked up the cry on the other side of the park, "*Call for doctors!*"

Asta and Najat saw a young boy emerge from behind the library, running beside the lane and still yelling for help. Najat's hands felt solid around Asta's shoulders. The pain in her chest disappeared as she realized that it wasn't her own.

"Najat!" she said. He snapped to face her so immediately, and his eyes fell upon her so intensely, she thought it must be improper to address him by name. She swallowed and said, "Kumasagi . . . Your Eminence . . ." Her eyes begged him to tell her what was happening.

He spread one hand over the side of her face to smooth away matted strands of hair and clinging tears. Barely visible through the trees behind him, several doctors and aides dashed through the park toward the library. The young boy still hopped on alternating feet at the corner, acting as a beacon. "*Doctors! To the Boys School!*"

Najat said to Asta, "They are too late." He closed his eyes and tilted his head. "Mahasagi doesn't know—he is in deep with the other patient."

Then Najat bent to pick up Asta's splayed sketchbook, found the pencil, and thrust them both into her hands. "Come with me." He took her arm and pulled her toward the Mahasagi's annex. When they got there, Asta realized that he didn't mean to go inside—he had simply chosen the shortest route to the water lane.

He turned to her and held her shoulders square. "It's coming from the Boys School. You Felt it. Now you must clear your mind. I need you to clear your mind and clear your heart."

Asta nodded and took a deep breath. Najat wriggled out of his silk vest and untied the deep blue sash at his waist and removed his loose pants and handed it all to Asta. Then he unclipped the silver cuffs from his ankles, threw them on top of the pile in her arms, and said, standing tall and lean in only his loincloth, "Meet me there."

He dove into the water. Asta stared after him, suddenly reminded how often she had looked for him in the lane when the divers swam beneath the windows of the nursery. She had looked for him before she even knew him.

She watched until he disappeared with a final, sun-sparkled splash behind the landscaped garden of the library. Then she took a moment to breathe again and folded his clothes into a neat stack. She tucked the stack above her sketchbook and the ankle cuffs into a pocket of her tunic. She tried very hard to clear her mind as he had asked.

She knew where to find the Boys School. She had accompanied Jayan on his favorite walking route from the university once or twice, and he always pointed things out along the way. That route took them by the swim training venues and the Boys School bath house, and she had been impressed by the grand structure of the school itself rising against the sky behind the smaller buildings.

This time she followed Najat's route, because the doctors and the beacon boy had also disappeared in that direction. The library stood near Amala Vengar's wing of the nursery, with the nursery wall and water lane to separate them. Asta hurried through that juncture, then saw the Boys School loom before her, almost as tall as the temple. The lane passed directly through the center of the building, cutting through a grand archway in the ground level.

Asta stepped along the lane to the archway and entered a short tunnel, where a lone man stood comforting two young boys. He stopped Asta and whispered, "We cannot allow visitors at this time. Please come back later."

Asta dipped Najat's clothing toward the man. "For the Kumasagi," she said. "I must be on hand."

Both boys stared up at her with shiny eyes and tear-streaked cheeks. The man said, "Apologies, Saati. You will see him on the left. Please go softly."

"Of course!" Asta shot him a look, appearing more offended than she felt. Inwardly, she thanked herself for not stuttering.

The man gave a sheepish nod and gestured through the arch.

A din of young voices met her ear as she approached the other side of the tunnel. An immense grass and dirt courtyard opened before her, split perfectly down the middle by the water lane. Chattering boys of every age, shape, and size milled across the right side of the courtyard as their elders herded them with scooping hands and low, insistent commands. "Quietly! Keep moving!"

Asta glanced up to the towering inner walls of the complex and saw several adults herding more boys along the open balconies and down the steps. They all moved in the same direction, toward the southern archways far to

Asta's right. She knew those paths must lead to the swim training venues. Asta realized that this main part of the complex—most likely the dormitory and classrooms—was being evacuated.

Within minutes the courtyard stood empty and silent, save for a limping trickle of water from an old, crack-fissured fountain to the right of the lane. Asta walked over a footbridge to the left side of the lane and saw a group of adults huddled at the far end of the yard, almost tiny at that distance.

One of the adults—a doctor—noticed Asta picking her way through the demarcated exercise and play areas, and walked out to meet her. Barren climbing gyms and exposed foot game mosaics echoed with the eerie absence of children, a silence cut only by the trickling water and the thinly pitched, wailing sobs of a single boy.

"Gampo-Saati," the doctor greeted her midway. He knew her from her recent visits with the children at Medical Arts. "What are you doing here?"

"Pana-Saat," she greeted him. "I was speaking—I was speaking with His Eminence when we heard the—the—the signal. He asked me to—he asked me to—to—to bring his clothes."

"I see." Doctor Panarajan's height put him eye to eye with Asta, and his build was of a similar weight. She remembered meeting him for the first time in Medical Arts—she had been charmed by his straightforward manner and cheerfully dimpled face. Now his plump cheeks appeared droopy and ashen.

"What happened?" she asked him.

Doctor Panarajan exhaled a morose grunt. "A child fell

from the fifth floor," he said, pointing far above the huddled group of adults. "The fall killed him."

Asta clutched Najat's clothes to her chest, feeling a sudden ache again. It faded just as quickly.

"I would like to join you," she said.

The doctor hesitated.

"*Please.*"

He finally nodded, knowing what she had seen among the patients in Medical Arts.

He led Asta to the others, near the balustrade of the ground-level walkway. The wailing and sobbing grew louder, but still distant, and she looked up, realizing the sound came from the fifth floor above. Two small hands clung to the rails of the banister. She could see an adult kneeling beside the hands.

The doctor whispered to her, "A friend witnessed the incident."

They stepped onto a stonework patio accented with decorative blue tiles. The doctor tugged Asta's arm to halt her several paces from the site of the fall, where three adults stood with bowed heads—two of them wearing medical jackets with the same green collar as Doctor Panarajan's, and one apparently a staff member of the school. A fourth, older man stood with head up, throwing dark glances around the complex and a penetrating look at Asta. She guessed he must be the school director.

A fifth figure crouched unmoving at the feet of the others . . . Najat. Asta's throat clenched and tears sprang to her eyes at the sight of him. Water drizzled down his bare limbs to soak the white cotton pants of a small boy. The boy's limp, broken body rested in Najat's arms, with his hair spread in moistened, pale curls against Najat's dark chest. Asta gazed from Najat's bent head to the closed eyes of the boy, and imagined that the boy could simply be in a nap, if he didn't have that thin, terribly dark stream of blood connecting the corner of his mouth to the corner of his dripping chin.

"*Be-maran*," Doctor Panarajan spoke quietly beside her. *Untimely death.*

Asta noticed subtle red streaks on Najat's arms and a few red droplets spangling his knees, just as she also noticed the sound of someone running up from behind, and the sound of someone screaming. Najat flinched, but his eyes remained closed. Asta twirled around and blocked the boy's mother with one hip and a firm grasp on the panicked woman's shoulder.

"Ayal! Ayal!" The woman screamed her son's name over and over as the doctor and Asta wrestled her back, step by step, trying to move her a reasonable distance from the Kumasagi. The school's director left Najat's side and approached the mother at a deliberate angle to block the boy from her sight.

Najat felt a ray of hot sunlight strike his face as the director stepped away. The sensation faded as Najat sank inward again, struggling to guard the boy's terrified consciousness from the mother's screams and grasping kana. Najat bubbled a massively thick shield around his own living body and the lifeless weight in his arms, so that no sights, sounds or outside emotions could disturb them. The two doctors and the school aide stepped back, pushed by an unknown, instinctive need to relieve a dull pressure in their heads.

After restabilizing himself, Najat resumed his attempts to communicate with the boy. The terrible impact had jolted the boy out of his physical body, yet he still carried physical pain as a mental projection in his disembodied state. The projection was strong, enveloping the boy's kana in a crackling latticework of confusion and terror. Najat sensed the latticework thickening to a black crust as the boy's mind screamed from within it.

Najat kept his own mind free of any thoughts or panic. He entered a state of meditation so deep that he lost all sense of himself, save for the clearest central core of his own kana, which opened up towards the trapped boy like a flower opening its petals to the sun.

The flower-like core produced its own light, illuminating the dark and tangled crust of the boy's hardening fear. The calm, soft light penetrated the latticed barrier without breaking it, and glided through the boy's confused mental screams without silencing them. The light held no consciousness or purpose of its own. It could not search out, or find, or alter the boy's confused state. It simply emanated and expanded, clear and strong and unchanging.

Even as the light had no awareness of the boy, the boy slowly came aware to the light. Something deep inside of him—something that existed beyond pain and fear— resonated in response to the calm, clear essence that permeated his awareness. The boy's mental screams dwindled to a whimper, then to a wisp of nothingness as his consciousness divided from the emotional constructs that had trapped him.

A fissure split the latticework. The boy spilled out of his

cage in an exhausted heap, unable to remember his previous form and immediately losing any concern about it. The current landscape offered a view of black, starlit outer space above him, and a field of pale yellow grass far below. His hovering form rested somewhere between, never knowing that what glowed below him was the outer skin of Ayudena the Skyfish. The latticework crumbled and dissipated behind him, already forgotten.

A figure appeared before him, tall and semi-transparent, formed of a self-emanating, deep blue light. The boy flowed toward the figure and felt something else within that liquid blue—something that wasn't light at all, but somehow felt brighter and more clear than anything else from any remembered realm of consciousness. The boy fell forward and grasped what couldn't be grasped, and smelled it and tasted it and tuned to the nonexistent vibrations of it, slipping into a merged state so suddenly that he possessed no self to comprehend his own last thought: *I am bliss.*

The blue figure staggered backward—heavy, off balance, dimming and sparking and fizzing.

Najat's physical body remained motionless on the hard stone patio, even as sudden beads of sweat mingled with the droplets of water on his skin. He fought to maintain the trance deep inside himself, even as his mind tugged him outward: *This shouldn't happen! I did something wrong!* He had meant to shield his inner kana after using it to draw out the boy, and then stay as a guide, as a Mahasagi should—

But he had failed to protect himself. The fathomless pain pulled him back in—intensely personal, emotional, disorienting. The boy's kana melded to him like hot wax.

Najat's ethereal body fell to one knee above the sea of sun-colored grass. Darkening shadows sucked across the horizon, until the edge of his awareness appeared stained and murky.

Several figures stepped out from the gloom, their forms solidifying to smooth gray silhouettes against the darker atmosphere. They stood before Najat without showing any concern. He knew they were *devadutas*, the companions of Ayudena the Skyfish. He had sensed them during his deepest meditations. Even as his inner vision blurred and faded, he comprehended five devadutas surrounding him now.

He knew that communicating with them could be very difficult.

Ideas came to him, transmitted to Najat from the devadutas as if in the place of words. One of the entities stepped closer. They knew he had committed a terrible blunder. Yet a sense of respect flowed into him from these beings, a sense that they knew something more about Najat than he himself did. They flooded his wracked ethereal body with smooth, almost tangible placidity, similar to the calm light he had emanated for the boy.

The four flanking devadutas lifted Najat to his feet, not so much with their hands, but with a transmitted urge for him to stand. His consciousness stretched wide, as a physical man might yawn and throw back his arms—but this widening gripped Najat with an incredible, pulling pain, causing more sparking and fizzing. He could not hold back his own mental screams. Every part of him felt fused, crusted, gummy.

The main devaduta thrust its shapeless hands into Najat

and began sifting through the stretched membranes of light to magnetize the dispersed kana of the boy.

Najat screamed again—even as his physical body knelt silent and still on the patio. He writhed in the spongy soft, steadfast grip of the flanking devadutas. The central entity maintained its connection to the boy, accumulating the boy's kana as it ripped apart from Najat piece by piece. Najat's ethereal body shuddered and convulsed, even as he caught a vague sense that

:: helping ::

the devadutas were trying to communicate.

:: helping you ::

The tranquilizing placidity flooded in again. Najat rested amid the pain, trying to cooperate. His inner senses cleared again, which brought the pain into focus but also allowed him to center and stabilize himself.

:: greater ::

He struggled to understand. The central entity still hovered close, with its hands buried inside of him. The pain only seemed to grow.

:: greater. larger. ::

They needed something . . . they needed his help. Najat felt that sense of respect coming from them again, and it bolstered him. The flanking devadutas lightened their touch at his shoulders and arms.

:: kumasagi. you must. BE. ::

He finally understood, at which moment all understanding and attempts at thought vanished. His ethereal body dissolved in the grasp of the four flanking devadutas as his inner kana expanded, enveloping and dwarfing the devadutas instantaneously.

Without thought, without emotion, the true essence of the Kumasagi left nothing for the boy's kana to latch onto. The boy's consciousness merged back into itself, becoming a beautiful shakti cradled in the steady arms of the main devaduta. The five devadutas rested at the softly bright center of an immense sphere of blue light.

The landscape changed as Najat came back to his inner senses, forming back into his radiant blue ethereal body. The stars twinkled on again, and there were so many, visible to such great depths, that the black universe above him appeared blotched with silver and gray. His home world spun slowly below him, but Ayudena the Skyfish— covered in so many scales that it appeared as a field of waving, yellow grass—blocked his view of it.

Najat could sense the boy's shakti as it rested in the arms of the central devaduta. The five devadutas relayed a single notion to Najat: This little one had not been harmed.

Najat brought a glowing blue hand to his chest— something still turned inside of him, something that wasn't his own. The devadutas had completely extracted the boy, Najat was sure of it. He felt something else . . . a shimmering sphere of kana marbled with color, similar to the shaktis he had Seen and Felt so many times at the lake. He directed a questioning thought to the main entity, and received an answer. The devadutas had sensed the marbled orb while retrieving the boy, but chose to leave it alone. It was a living light, and therefore no concern of theirs.

Asta. This was a wisp of Asta's kana, existing inside of him all this time. Najat held both hands over his ethereal chest. A flush of joy seeped over him, but his first concern was the boy.

The devadutas stepped back. Najat bowed to them, and although they did not return any bows or gestures, he felt their high regard. The devadutas held the boy's transformed consciousness and floated down until they disappeared below the waving scales, into the Skyfish, where Najat could not follow.

He turned to see Mahasagi Tebhan hovering next to him. He Felt the Mahasagi's stern command to return home.

Sunlight struck Najat's face again, and he became aware of the weight in his arms. The weight decreased as his muscles flexed and his eyes fluttered open. Ayal's head rolled away from Najat's chest and landed at a grotesque angle, stamping his own breast with a chin print of blood. Najat gazed down at the small crumpled body and cradled it with one arm so he could use his other hand to lift the boy's head back against the crook of his elbow.

"Ayal!" the boy's mother cried. Najat looked up to see her standing between the school's director and Doctor Panarajan. He reabsorbed the heavy shield and felt everything snap into focus around him—the warm stone under his bare feet, the smell of blood and water, the sun-heated breeze against his wet skin.

Nearer to Najat, but slightly off to the side, two medical aides knelt by an adult-sized white stretcher. Najat swallowed against a suddenly dry throat. He met the eyes of the nearest aide and made a lifting gesture with his full arm. The aides rushed forward and positioned the stretcher in front of Najat.

He felt the child's bones grind together as he moved to lay the body on the stretcher. He took special care to make sure the tiny broken head and neck did not tilt again, but instead rested in a peaceful, centered pose against the rough cotton fabric.

Then Najat stood up, his own joints creaking, and stepped back as the mother rushed in.

The director approached him as he stood there in his loincloth, still streaked with water and blood, flexing his cramped hands and testing his lips with his dry tongue.

"The father is on business in the valley," the director said. "We've sent a flier."

Najat spoke with a forced croak. "I will ask . . . His Eminence to pay a visit . . . when the father returns." He looked to the mother, who had bent herself between the hovering medical team and the calm form of her dead son, weeping so hard that it came out almost silent.

"The child is at peace," Najat told the director.

The director nodded, but Najat knew the man had little understanding of what the boy had just endured.

"They were playing on the rail," the director said. "We haven't determined how they went unnoticed. We will conduct interviews . . ." His focus drifted inward, to his own thoughts.

"Please let the family know that we will visit," Najat said.

"Yes, of course. And thank you . . . I suppose the Mahasagi was not available?"

Najat's shoulders felt heavy. "He was not available."

He sensed someone at his elbow and turned to see the school attendant holding an armful of towels, with Asta right beside her. *Asta!* Najat stepped toward her, but then stopped himself as Asta broke eye contact with him and nodded politely at the director. The director nodded in return and then left to attend to the mother.

Asta found Najat's eyes again and held up a large cup of water. He grabbed it from her and gulped down the water until it was gone.

"Do you need more?"

He shook his head, handed back the cup, and started breathing again. The drink had cleared his head as well as his throat. He took a towel from the other woman, soaked it with water and sweat from his skin, then used that to wipe away the boy's blood.

He handed back the towel with a nod of gratitude, then walked with Asta to the opposite side of a large climbing gym. She handed him his clothes one piece at a time and showed no alarm as he fumbled with his sash. She reached in and tucked in the ends for him. His own hands felt thick, and his shoulders increasingly leaden.

Asta's beautiful, open face looked up at him. Her light gray eyes were rimmed in pink, but he saw no tears. "Are you alright?" he asked her.

She kept her voice low. "I'm fine. Are *you* alright?"

He shook his head. "I need to leave this place."

Asta turned without question and led him to the water lane. She stopped to look through the western tunnel where she had come in, and even as Najat thought how he didn't want to walk back that way—where they would pass near Vengar's side of the nursery—Asta made a decision of her own and led him over the nearest bridge toward the school's south exits.

The clamoring voices of school boys echoed from the first and second swimming pools across the wider lane outside of the school. Asta detoured down an alley between the library and the third, empty pool. Najat kept pace immediately behind her as she slipped through a gap in the low wall around the Mahasagi's private garden.

"Gampo-Saati," Najat said from above her left ear. His hand scooped into the crook of her elbow, slowing her headstrong march toward the Mahasagi's annex. She had not been sure of what else to do, or where else to take him— suddenly Asta remembered that it might not be appropriate for her to enter the Kumasagi's private quarters.

Najat's other hand closed over her shoulder, and she realized that he was leaning on her for support. "Asta . . . let's sit for a moment . . ."

She walked with careful balance under his weight, until they reached a stone bench that was littered with fallen tree blossoms. She brushed the crusty flowers aside and helped Najat sit down. His fingers remained around her arm.

He took a slow breath in and let a slow breath out. "The boy . . . Ayal. He is at peace," he said.

Asta nodded, not sure what to say. Najat's hand felt fluid against her skin, even as he gripped her tighter. He seemed to shimmer and blur beside her, consumed by a liquid halo of blue light, which she could somehow See, though not with her eyes.

Now Asta understood—his shield was down.

"You don't seem well," she said without hearing herself. A wisp of a memory snaked across her senses—a ripping sensation down her sternum—droplets of glowing blue water against dark, copper-flecked skin—

—a hut on a beach, where the waves limped to shore on a calm, sunny day—an older boy with bronze skin shaking her shoulder and then running away again—

"Thank you for your help, Gampoban-Saati," said a gravelly voice over her shoulder. "Do you need a ride to Patal?"

Asta jumped. The Mahasagi's Second Hand stood right next to the bench, his block-like face angled down at her from far above. Najat dropped his hand from Asta's numb arm and slid apart from her on the bench.

Asta stood up and shuffled around Rajung's massive arm. "Just—just—just going back to Medical Arts," she mumbled. "I can walk. I like to walk." She clutched her sketchbook to her chest and executed a quick bow and mudra toward Najat. "Kumasagi."

She saw Najat press his hands together in a mudra of blessing before Rajung stepped between them and blocked her view.

Walking through the park, Asta tried to regain the vision that Rajung had startled out of her head. It was too disjointed, like the memory of a dream. It fell away in pieces until she entered the mosaic courtyard of the Medical Arts building, already forgetting that she had Felt or Seen it at all.

~ CHAPTER 15 ~

Asta did not sleep well that night, alone in Jayan's dark university apartment. Finally she rose from the low bed, slid back the wall screens of the bedroom, and stepped down into the sunroom to light the wall lamps. Their yellow glow illuminated her only companions—stacks upon stacks of specimen boxes left by Jayan around the hulking form of the *Swallowtail.* He still hadn't managed to get all of it organized and transferred over to the horticulture building.

She crossed into the kitchen, stuck an arm out of the blanket she had wrapped around herself, and pressed her hand against the slab of blackrock under the window. Its dull warmth would not be sufficient to start a pot for tea. She cranked the slab up to its heating position above the window sill.

There was nothing to see beyond the open window, save for a sliver of gray where the black silhouette of distant mountains met a predawn sky. Asta gazed into that nothingness and thought of the dead boy, smashed against the stone patio, then pressed against the Kumasagi's tender sternum.

Something in the boy's death had affected Najat. He had become vulnerable afterward—she remembered his shimmering grip on her arm and the liquid light that poured out of his bent form. But somehow she couldn't remember how that light *felt*. She only remembered Rajung standing over her, and then Rajung standing over the Kumasagi as she fled with her precious sketchbook and fuzzed-up thoughts.

It bothered her, not knowing what had happened to Najat after that.

She wandered around the room and thought to distract herself with a book—she should probably be reading Jayan's published journals, but her reading skills couldn't keep up with such academic works. She found a thin, faded green book stuffed along the top of others on a shelf, and opened it to find printed illustrations of various mythical creatures, such as the terrifying, fish-like destins that some people thought could be found in the wild, which could hypnotize a man and drag him to his death underwater.

She opened several more books from the same shelf and found more illustrations and texts on the subject of wild destins.

A dim, mechanical chime from the front room startled Asta. She turned her head slightly as someone cranked the doorbell turnkey again, and for a slim moment she actually thought it might be Rajung, on a thug's mission to make sure she never went near the Kumasagi again.

Asta shook that absurd thought out of her head. She

padded back through the bedroom, changing from the blanket to a proper dressing gown along the way. She paused in the hallway, until the turnkey chimed again. Finally she lit a wall lamp in the front room and peered through a small peephole in the front door.

She opened the door immediately. Najat stood there like an apparition of darkness, with a gloomy hooded cloak covering his head and most of his face. His figure seemed to fade into the murky street behind him, even as he stood mere inches from the threshold of Asta's door. The sight of him caused a hot flush from her forehead to her throat.

His voice came out strangely diluted, as if strained through a deep tunnel of wind. "May I come in?"

Asta regained her breath and gestured for Najat to come inside. He nudged his way to an open spot among the specimen boxes and lab equipment piled in the front room as she shut the door.

"Kumasagi, are you alright?"

He dropped the hood of his cloak to a puddle around his shoulders and smiled down at Asta. The lamplight solidified his smooth scalp and face so suddenly that Asta thought she must have imagined the shimmering effect when he was outside the door. Even his voice returned to its full weight. "Yes, thank you. Thank you for letting me see you so early."

"This *is* an—an—an unusual time . . ."

"I'm sorry, Gampoban-Saati, but I need to speak with you—"

"You are always welcome." She looked right up into his eyes to make sure he understood. "I just want—I just want—I just—" She paused and took a breath. "I want to know that you're alright. Yesterday . . ."

"Yesterday . . . was difficult. I'd like to know that *you're* alright."

"Yes, I am well."

They stood there for a moment, until Asta realized from Najat's tightened expression that he hadn't come all the way down to Patal University at this time of the morning just to find out if she was well.

She dropped her eyes and gestured again, this time toward the narrow hallway. "I don't have tea yet, but I can—but I can—I can offer you some cakotara juice."

He followed her to the back of the apartment, where a long wall of windows in the sunroom glowed softly white from the gathering sunlight.

"It will only take a moment," she said from the open kitchen. "Please, sit."

Within minutes she joined him at the table in the sunroom with two small glasses of fresh-squeezed juice. "There's tari oil," she said, indicating with a webbed finger stretched out from her glass. Attempting, against all caution and shyness, to search him with an open line, she smacked into a shield so thick that she fumbled for a sip of juice to cover her surprise. Najat seemed to be surrounded by a wall of glass bricks, much more dense and impenetrable than the thin, ice-like glaze she had sensed the day before.

He wet his fingers with oil from the ceramic jar and rubbed it over his hands and the scales above his wrists. He glanced up at Asta as he replaced the lid and said, "Rajung thinks he might have startled you yesterday."

"Rajung?" Asta's stomach felt tight.

"The Mahasagi's Second Hand. He met us in the orchard

yesterday."

"I know who he is. And he *did* startle me. Wasn't that his—his—his intention?"

"He didn't expect you to leave so quickly," Najat said. His lips quirked, setting off an angled crease from one corner of his mouth. "Rajung doesn't always realize the effect that his . . . size and demeanor have on others."

"Should I have stayed?"

"No, it's alright. You were a great help to me yesterday. When Rajung thanked you, he was sincere."

Asta adjusted herself on her cushion, took a deep breath, and said, "Please forgive me, but you seemed unwell after—after—after the—the—the boy's accident. Does that always happen after—does that always happen after you attend someone's death?" She felt nervous asking the Kumasagi such a question.

Najat pushed his glass of juice aside, folded his hands to his lap, and leaned forward. "I've only attended three others before that, and all with the Mahasagi present. I was exhausted after each one, but he said the stamina for it grows with experience." Najat's brows dropped low. "Yesterday was different—and much more difficult— because of the boy's trauma, and I had decided to act on my own . . ."

Asta gripped her own glass with both hands, barely daring to breathe. She had never heard Najat speak so many words at a time, and certainly not from such a personal view. She was afraid any movement would cause him to stop.

"The boy, Ayal . . . his transfer ended well," Najat said. "Very well for him, I know it. But I wish he could have been saved—the doctors tried. The Mahasagi can only ease the transference of kana back to its shakti form . . . we cannot heal physical wounds of the body."

Then he did stop. Asta ventured to ask, "What did the Mahasagi say when he learned of it?"

"I don't know. I saw him for only a moment after Rajung took me back, and then I fell asleep . . . which may have been Tebhan's doing. I woke up in the middle of the night with my strength returned. But I have a sense that he will send me on another retreat today."

"Retreat?"

"More learning, practice, meditation. It would be at the Shakti Lake hut or the one down by Thin River—but here or there, I'll be in seclusion for half a tenday or more. That's why I came to see you now. Only one other person knows that I'm here."

"His Eminence . . . ?" Asta felt sudden slivers of jealousy over the deep, mystical bond that the old Mahasagi shared with Najat. A flush of shame swept the slivers away just as quickly.

"I'm not sure if *he* knows," Najat said. "Some things . . . are not spoken between us. But Rajung guessed where I might be going and insisted on coming with me. I know he acted on his own, not on orders from the Mahasagi."

"Rajung is here?!"

"Standing watch outside."

"Isn't he—won't he be—won't he be conspicuous standing out there?" She could picture Rajung blocking the door with his trunk-like legs planted far apart and his branch-like arms bent to plant his rocky knuckles on his boulder-like hips. His thick neck would be thrust forward, showing off his most intimidating face to anyone passing by.

Najat smiled. "He is invisible at the moment."

Asta closed her mouth. She remembered Najat's own faded form when he stood outside the front door. She knew that Amalas and divers could enter trances so clear that their bodies and minds became invisible to newborn destins—and she had heard that some of the greater mystics could make themselves invisible to anyone else.

Najat watched Asta grow very still in her seat across the table. Her white hair was still mussed from her attempt to sleep earlier in the night, and several locks had escaped their usual place behind her ears. She made no move to tuck the curls away from her eyes, but instead gazed right through them. "Why are you here?" she asked.

Najat felt his mental shield waver, but only for the spare amount of time it took him to straighten his spine and feed a little more energy into the barrier. Asta might no longer be a pashi destin, but her presence still pulled at him. He felt wary of his own thoughts as he spoke.

"Yesterday, when the boy fell, you sensed it," he said. "Has that ever happened to you before?"

Her shoulders dropped a scant measure, and her face softened as she gave it some thought. "No. I thought it happened because I was with you . . . and—and—and . . . you're the Kumasagi . . ."

He shook his head. "I don't think that would do it. Have you Felt anything from the patients in Medical Arts? Their illnesses, or improving health . . . ?"

"Maybe . . . but so much of that can be told from just—from just—just from the sight of them, or talking—or from talking with them."

"Are you able to See the Ayudena—the Skyfish—when it appears over the lake?"

"Yes."

"Do you See the shaktis—or Feel them in any way—before they arrive?"

"Yes." Asta's posture stiffened again.

Najat wrapped a broad hand over his smooth scalp and crinkled his eyes. "I'm sorry for all these questions. It's not . . . common for someone other than myself or the Mahasagi to sense be-maran." He tapped restless fingers against the table top. "Have they ever asked you to serve in the nursery?"

She paused before answering, "No. I can Feel and See the shaktis, and the Ayudena. But I can't—can't—can't go near the destins. I can't stabilize a clear trance."

"Ah," Najat rumbled.

"They tried to—they tried to train me. Amala Tebbe was very patient . . . but I just couldn't do it."

"Is that something you *wanted* to do?"

Asta thought of her precious drawings crushed under Amala Vengar's arm. "Maybe I wouldn't want to serve in the nursery. But I still wish I had—I wish I—I—I had shown some progress, for all of Amala Tebbe's effort."

Najat shook his head. "Amala wouldn't be disappointed by that. Do you know Maore Natarajan, Mathin's mother? She is the same. She can See the Ayudena and the shaktis, but her life's work is not in the nursery. And she has remained a great friend to Amala."

Asta lifted her eyes up to his, and they shared a quiet moment of understanding. Najat—who had received initiations and training from Amala Tebbe in his youth, and loved the old Amala completely—could see how Asta's love for Tebbe also ran very deep.

He felt a twinge in his sternum that was certainly a nudge from Rajung. "Thank you for the juice," he said to Asta, although his glass was not empty. He shifted his legs over the floor cushions. "I must return to the plateau."

Asta shifted on her own cushion across the table. "What does it mean, if I sensed—if I—if I—if I sensed Ayal's death on my own?"

Najat paused and rested one dark forearm on an upraised knee. "I don't know yet. The Mahasagi and Kumasagi are not the only ones who can perform *carhana*—guiding the soul back to the Ayudena—even if the temple would like it to seem that way. Amala Tebbe has performed carhana, and a select few other Amalas, past and present. You're not an Amala, but you can sense be-maran."

Asta shook her head. "That's the only—that's—that's the only time it's happened. You were with me. That must be why—"

"Asta, you have certain gifts beyond your ability to draw. I knew it before yesterday."

Asta's skin flushed bright red from her collarbone to her hairline.

Najat Felt her flush as much as he saw it. He looked down at his ankle and expelled a slow breath. "Perhaps others—who aren't the Mahasagi or Kumasagi or an Amala—could be trained in certain aspects of carhana guidance, even if they can't reach the Ayudena like we can." He stumbled on, suddenly apologetic, "You have a life here with Jayan. I don't expect you to train under the Mahasagi.

But please let me know if you have any . . . ah . . . extrasensory experiences involving the patients in Medical Arts. This information would be helpful to . . . to me."

"I did sense something else yesterday."

A shiver ran along Najat's forearms, lifting his wrist scales up row by row. He brought his knee down, put his webbed hands in his lap, and sat very still.

"In the orchard, before Rajung arrived," Asta continued, "I felt a—I felt a—I felt a—a—a sort of blue light, all around us . . . it was coming out of *you*. You had tremendous energy pouring out of you, and then I Saw something—I Saw something inside of it, a—a—a sort of vision—"

"You can see why I require more training," Najat said. "The boy's transfer was successful, but it took a great amount of effort for me. It left me . . . in a weakened state. Of course you would sense it—you have that gift."

"What *was* it that I sensed?" she asked. She paused for a cautious moment. Najat pressed his lips into a solid line and stared at her.

She stared right back. "It felt *familiar*," she said. "Like—like a—like a memory."

Najat mentally ran through a list of answers that might deflect her train of questions. All those fake answers jumbled together in his mind as he felt the tugging in his sternum, and finally he knew that it wasn't Rajung. It was Asta's stolen orb of kana, spinning and glowing inside of him.

Asta clutched her hands together and continued, "I also sensed something the first time we met, in the Mahasagi's audience room. I Felt you reaching towards me—you never—you never spoke of it, so I thought I—I—I just imagined . . ."

Najat's face contorted. That had been a careless indulgence on his part. He wrestled with that guilty thought even as Asta's kana swelled inside of him, threatening to overwhelm his carefully constructed shield.

She mistook his expression for one of shock and distaste. "So I . . . I did just imagine it?"

"No," he said. "You did not imagine it. But I shouldn't have done it."

Asta's heart started beating so hard that Najat could Feel every pulse from across the table. "But *why* did you do it? In the nursery, I used to have dreams about you. Before that day we met, I already *knew* you. Did you have the same dreams?"

Najat stood up. Asta jumped up to maintain eye contact with him. She swept her hand to indicate Jayan's apartment. "This was a mistake, wasn't it?" she said. "It wasn't supposed to be him!"

"Asta!"

"It's my fault. I saw him in the crowd and I thought he was you. I was looking for *you*. I made a mistake!"

One tear streaked down her flushed cheek. Her kana spun inside of Najat, driving him to the brink of dizziness. He spread his hand over his sternum and took another slow breath. He knew he had to stop this, right here and now.

"Asta," he said in his calmest booming voice. He felt the floor against the soles of his bare feet and centered the shield around himself. "We are not meant to be together. The Kumasagi cannot take a wife."

Three more tears came in quick succession.

"Not even the Mahasagi can take a wife."

"The Amalas can have a mate—why not the Mahasagi?" she said. "Amala Tebbe had a—had—had a husband, and they had a son . . ."

Najat shook his head with a patient smile. "That is just how it is. In any case, you know that I am second born."

The conventional wisdom about second sons— stemming from historical texts and teachings about the decline of the city of Ayunath—would be useful here, and he knew he must reinforce it for Asta . . . even if he had stopped believing it himself the day that he met the pashi destin tagged with blue. What he said next was such a lie that he had to divert half of his own attention by pressing his toes hard against the floor, just to say out loud to Asta, "I am not . . . capable of physical intimacy."

Asta blushed again and averted her eyes.

"But you are right," Najat said. "We *are* connected. I had several dreams of you as well. But it's only because—"

Rajung walked into the sunroom then, startling Asta as he came around from behind her to face them both.

She realized he must have been listening from the hallway. She blurted at him, "Let us finish our—our—our—our—our conversation, at least!"

Her remark simply bounced off Rajung. He wore a cloak similar to Najat's, and it made him appear even more mountainous as his shadow fell over Asta. His short white hair stood up in a wiry halo against the brightening windows in the background. His ice-blue eyes seemed to glow from his wide, backlit face as he stared at Najat.

Najat said, "I want her to know."

Rajung grunted and his eyes narrowed. Najat held his gaze for a long moment, as Asta held her breath. Rajung let out another low grunt, then finally turned and said to Asta, "What do you know about the circumstances of your birth?"

Asta hesitated. When she looked back at Najat, his expression urged her to answer Rajung.

Rajung spoke with a gentler tone, "Did Amala Tebbe or Selda Matirajan ever tell you about your birth?"

"There was a virus," Asta said. "My sisters fell ill before—before—before diksha, but they recovered. I also fell ill, but I did not recover. I became . . . slow."

"You are *not* slow," Najat said.

Rajung lifted a warning hand to Najat. Then he gestured for them both to sit down, and he joined them there on the floor beside the table. Najat remained close beside Asta.

"Do you know where the virus came from?" Rajung asked.

Asta shook her head. Najat twisted a length of his cloak between clenched fingers.

"Did you know that the Kumasagi was a diver?"

Asta shook her head more slowly, embarrassed that she hadn't figured it out already from Najat's shaved head and swimmer's build.

"The virus came from the Kumasagi," Rajung said. "Rather, it came from Jayan Gampoban. Jayan was infected while returning from an expedition, and he passed it to the Kumasagi."

"I did not handle it well," Najat said. "I shouldn't have gone on the dive. I fell very ill, but I didn't let anyone know. I went on the dive—the day you were born. And it made everyone else sick."

"Including the destins?" Asta asked.

"It is true that your sisters were infected by the virus. But you were not."

Asta looked at him, and then looked at Rajung. Tesame and Selda had told her the virus was to blame for her slow development. Amala Tebbe had never refuted it.

Rajung said, "You did not fall ill as they did. But there were . . . indirect consequences." He looked at Najat, thinking the Kumasagi would explain, but Najat's lips pressed into a tight line. As much as he wanted Asta to know of the events, Najat could not speak through a sudden swell of shame.

Rajung continued, "The Kumasagi was very sick after that dive. He could not hold a trance in his weakened state. When you were still pashi, you left the nursery pool on your own. In an odd turn of events, the two of you met."

Asta could not comprehend it. "But . . . Amala Tebbe?"

Rajung shook his head. "Before she could reach you, you initiated be-diksha with the Kumasagi."

Asta's arms began to tremble as Rajung's words settled over her. She burst into tears.

Najat flinched. Rajung patted the air with his hands and told Asta, "It is inevitable in that situation. No one blames you for it—"

"*I* am to blame," said Najat.

Rajung raised a hand in his direction again. Asta put her own hands over her face and growled, as low and guttural as her voice could go. She didn't want to cry in front of these two. A memory came up fast in the dark behind her hands. She could smell the grotto's cold air, and see the pulsing blue water light up beside her, and feel Najat's sweat on her skin.

No, no! She shook her head, slapped her own cheeks,

and then wrapped her arms over her head as if she could prevent the two men from looking at her.

"Who else knows?" she asked from under one elbow.

"Amala Tebbe and Selda arrived in time to save you both. Amala performed her own diksha with you to reverse the mental scarring as much as she could. Dechen and I were also there, and the Mahasagi knew of everything."

"But why didn't they tell me?!"

"Gampoban-Saati." Rajung leaned forward with a palm on each thigh, elbows cranked out to either side. His tone became severe. "They had to protect the Kumasagi. *No one* must know about this! Confirm it with Amala Tebbe if you must, but let that be the end of it. Do not speak to anyone, whether myself or Dechen, Selda or the Mahasagi—and certainly not anyone else. This *cannot* be discussed further."

The Kumasagi sat up straight, protesting through a silent line to Rajung—he had not intended this knowledge to be such a burden for Asta. Rajung ignored him.

"Why did you even tell me about it?" Asta said, dashing her knuckles across her wet cheeks.

Rajung indicated Najat with an open hand, then swiveled his hand to Asta. "There is a connection here. Now you know why. It was an accident, an unfortunate turn of events. No one is to blame. But it is a delicate matter that should be kept private. He is the Kumasagi, you understand."

Asta's shoulders dropped as she listened.

"You will always have this connection to the Kumasagi. You may find him to be a great friend. But his duty is to Shakti Lake Temple, and his character must not . . . be compromised. And you have your own duties, as a wife to

Jayan. You can ask Amala Tebbe herself—your union with Jayan was *not* a mistake."

Asta snapped her head to look at Rajung, wondering what he meant by that. He stared right back at her with his stern blue eyes and said, "You should never expect to be the Kumasagi's mate."

Her cheeks steamed. "I don't want to be the Kumasagi's mate!" she said, pushing herself up from the floor. Rajung and Najat stood up with her. Asta couldn't look at Najat. "I won't—I won't compromise anyone," she said to Rajung. "I'm glad you—I'm glad you—you—you told me about this. It explains many things."

She turned and walked back up the short hallway with a clear indication that they should follow. The three of them stopped at the front door, where she finally looked up at Najat. "I'm sorry for my outburst. I was just . . . confused. But now I understand everything."

With Rajung standing beside him, Najat could only nod his head with a gracious smile, as if all had been settled. Perhaps it had been settled, after all. But as he followed Rajung to the long porch of the university apartments, and heard Asta close the door behind them, he was startled to feel the connection severed so quickly. Asta's kana dwindled to a hard nutshell inside of him, even as his hand came up to grasp the empty air in front of his chest.

A mental tug from Rajung distracted him. They would need to go invisible again for the greater part of their walk back to the plateau, and it helped to connect with each other in the trance-like state. Najat covered his head with the hood of his cloak and followed Rajung up the dusty road.

The story continues in

Kumasagi, Part 2: Kandargiri

www.LesleeSheu.com

~ MAP ~

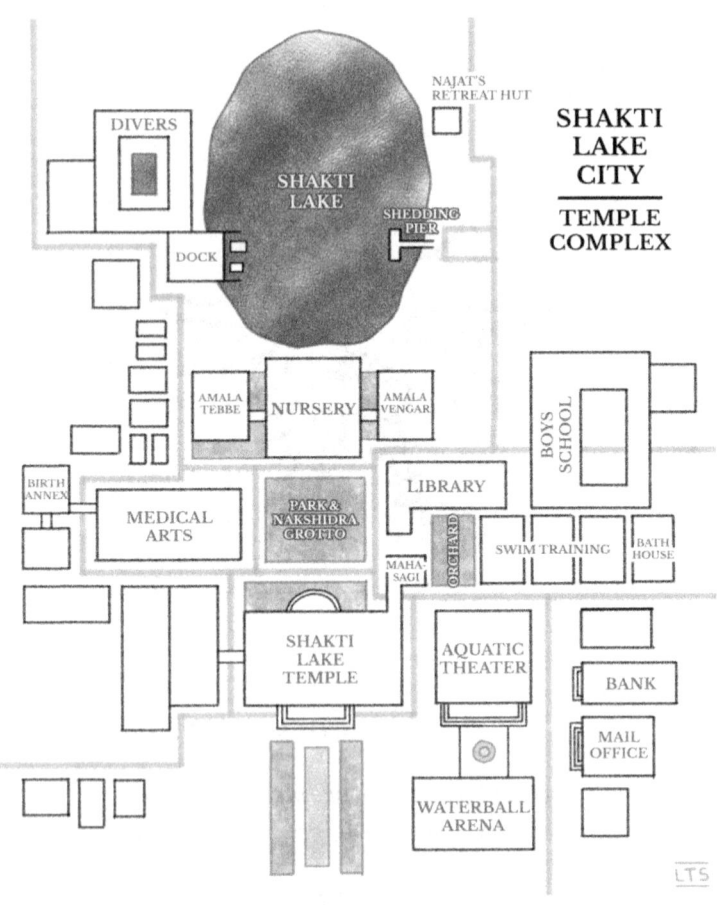

NAJAT'S
RETREAT HUT

SHAKTI
LAKE
CITY
───────
TEMPLE
COMPLEX

DIVERS

SHAKTI
LAKE

SHEDDING
PIER

DOCK

AMALA
TEBBE

NURSERY

AMALA
VENGAR

BOYS
SCHOOL

BIRTH
ANNEX

MEDICAL
ARTS

PARK &
NAKSHIDRA
GROTTO

LIBRARY

ORCHARD

SWIM TRAINING

BATH
HOUSE

MAHA'
SAGI

SHAKTI
LAKE
TEMPLE

AQUATIC
THEATER

BANK

MAIL
OFFICE

WATERBALL
ARENA

LTS

~ CHARACTER GUIDE ~

Shakti Lake City

Amala Tebbe – The older of two Amalas at Shakti Lake. Mahasagi Tebhan's mother.

Amala Vengar – The younger of two Amalas at Shakti Lake. Born in Kandargiri.

Asta Gampoban (Gampo-Saati, "Blue") – Artist, volunteer at Medical Arts. Jayan's wife.

Ayal – A boy who fell to his death from a fifth-story railing at the Boys School.

"Blue" – Asta's nickname when she was a nameless pashi destin. She had a blue ribbon tied around her wrist.

Cayman Natarajan (Nata-Saat) – The bursar of Shakti Lake Temple, who oversees the sale of destins. Maore's husband, Mathin's father.

Dechen Vrajanan – Mahasagi Tebhan's First Hand. Rajung's wife.

Doctor Panarajan – Head doctor at the children's ward of Medical Arts.

Fara – One of Amala Vengar's acolytes. Tesame's friend.

Gavind Sandarapan (Sandi) – Senior diver at Shakti Lake. Gavina and Aubik's son.

Kumasagi Najat – *See Najat Gampoban.*

Mahasagi Tebhan – A devaduta (angelic being) who lives in the body of a man. Currently, this holy manifestation is split between two men: Tebhan (the Mahasagi) and Najat (the Kumasagi). Tebhan is Amala Tebbe's son.

Maore Natarajan (Nata-Saati) – Head midwife at the maternity annex at Medical Arts. Cayman's wife, Mathin's mother.

Mathin Natarajan – Maore and Cayman's son.

Najat Gampoban – The only second child born in the last

few hundred years. He is the Kumasagi, which is the twin soul of the Mahasagi (*see Mahasagi Tebhan*). Formerly a senior diver at Shakti Lake. Jeniya and Delan's son, Jayan's brother.

Palen – Junior diver at Shakti Lake.

Rajung Vrajanan – Mahasagi Tebhan's Second Hand. Dechen's husband.

Ram – Senior diver at Shakti Lake.

Selda Matirajan (Big Selda) – Amala Tebbe's First Hand.

Seldan Matirajan – Selda's son.

Suchal – Teenager who works in his family's teahouse restaurant. Suchali's son.

Suchali – Owner of the Eastview Teahouse. Suchal's mother.

Tesame (Tez) – Amala Tebbe's Second Hand.

Vin – Senior diver at Shakti Lake.

Patal University

Dean Purnima Janipan (Dean Jani, Jani-Saati) – Dean of the Botany and Horticulture Department at Patal University. Purnil's mother.

Thin River Bend

Aubik Sandarapan – Blind potter. Gavina's husband, Gavind's father.

Gavina Sandarapan – Mosaic artist. Aubik's wife, Gavind's mother.

Dagaragiri / Blackrock Mines

Padir Dagarapan (Daga-Saat) – Owns the blackrock mines at Dagaragiri. He has a dangerous obsession with lopperbeaks. Sopani's husband, Sopan's father, Amala Mirigar's former lover.

Sopan Dagarapan – Sopani and Padir's son.
Sopani Dagarapan – Born in Kandargiri, now lives in Dagaragiri. Padir's wife, Sopan's mother.

Sindhupat Island

Delan Gampoban – Former Shakti Lake senior diver who now lives on the island. Jayan and Najat's father, Jeniya's widower.
Jayan Gampoban (Gampo-Saat) – Explorer with self-taught proficiencies in zoology, botany, and horticulture. Delan and Jeniya's first son, Najat's brother, Asta's husband.
Jeniya Gampoban – Endured giving birth to a second child (Najat), which damaged her health to the point that she died six years later. Delan's wife, Jayan and Najat's mother.

~ GLOSSARY ~

ama – Mother. A more affectionate form is "ama-la."

a'mama – Grandmother.

Amala – An honorific title that means "Revered Mother." *See diksha.*

a'pala – Grandfather.

Ayudena the Lifegiver (aka the Mighty Skyfish) – An extradimensional being which is the source of the shaktis, or life-spark, of the destins. It roams the upper atmosphere of the planet. Only mystics can "See" it or sense its presence. *See Skyfish.*

be-diksha – When a pashi destin mind-melds with someone who is not an Amala. This can mentally damage the destin and/or the victim. *See diksha.*

be-maran – Untimely death.

cakotara fruit – Similar to grapefruit.

carhana – The process of dying, when a person's kana transforms back into a shakti and returns to the Ayudena.

choli – Women's midriff-baring top with short sleeves.

destin – Each woman is born from an aquatic pod in a fresh water pool, lake, or cave grotto. Their bodies are grown from the earth but their life spark (shakti) comes from the Ayudena. A destin is an unmarried woman who still lives under the guardianship of a nursery.

devaduta – Angel-like companions/caretakers of the Ayudena.

diksha – One or more mental/spiritual initiations performed by an Amala to awaken the cognizance of a newly born destin, and to transfer a baseline of knowledge (especially speech/language).

dikshani – When an Amala performs diksha for a destin, the Amala becomes that destin's dikshani, and the destin becomes that Amala's daughter.

diver – A mystic who is specifically trained to protect his or her mind from a pashi destin. The divers are master swimmers. They retrieve (or "harvest") pashi destins that have just been born.

The Eight Cities – Ayunath, Dagaragiri, Gahvari Ghat, Kalan Town, Kandargiri, Orasarana, Shakti Lake City, Sindhupat Island.

fendel tree / fendelwood – The wood from this tree is traditionally used to make the boxes which hold the braided hair of newborn destins. The oils from the tree are used to make fendelwood incense.

flier(s) – A service that uses trained birds to carry written messages.

jawfish – When a person dies their body is typically lowered into a burial lake from a funeral barge. These scavenger fish consume the bodies of the dead.

kana – See *shakti*.

kuma- (prefix) – "Younger." Sometimes added before a young man's last name when addressed by an older person.

kuma-la – A term of endearment for a young boy, especially one's son.

Kumasagi – "Younger Mahasagi." As the Mahasagi gets older, his devaduta essence will split so that part of it manifests in a newborn boy. The boy who shares the essence of the Mahasagi is called the Kumasagi. When the Mahasagi dies, the essence from that body absorbs into the Kumasagi, making him "whole" again, and the Kumasagi becomes the Mahasagi.

-la (suffix) – Suffix added to a name as a term of endearment.

lopperbeak – Giant birds that nest in the cliffs at the edge of the Southern Sea.

Mahasagi – The Mahasagi is a revered mystic who has a profound connection to the Ayudena. He is one of the caretakers (devaduta) of the Ayudena, but he is the only devaduta who lives among people, incarnated in the body of a man. The Mahasagi's role is to ease any mental confusion or suffering as a person dies, and help their spirit (kana) transition back into a shakti and return to the Ayudena. *See Kumasagi.*

mountains – Achilagiri (Giant Mountain), Agalagiri (Second Mountain), Dagaragiri (named after Padir's ancestors), Duragiri (Far Away Mountain), Kandargiri (Cliff Mountain), Madhyagiri (Middle Mountain), Nichagiri (Flat Mountain), Shaktigiri (Spirit Mountain), Utaragiri (North Mountain).

mystic – A person who possesses powers of heightened awareness and empathy. This may come naturally or by intense training. Although mystics can communicate with each other by mentally conveying ideas, images, or emotions, they can't send words (such as with verbal telepathy).

Nakshidra – "Starlight vein." Each destin lake or pool has a Nakshidra grotto nearby, where the "blood of the earth" flows from the cave wall into a sacred pool, then back underground to nourish the destin pods in the nearby lake. The Nakshidra grottos are connected by a network of underground "veins."

pala – Father.

pashi – A pashi destin is a woman just born, who has not yet received initiation (diksha) by an Amala. Pashi destins instinctively search for someone to mind-meld with, and may try to do it with someone other than an Amala.

pedicab – A rickshaw-type transport, or even larger, that is pulled by a person (or persons) pedaling two, three, or more wheels.

podalcab – A rickshaw-type transport that is pulled by a person on foot.

runner – A person who can be hired to carry and deliver written messages. Flier stations employ runners to deliver messages brought in by the trained birds.

Saat – Honorific for men, especially when addressing someone older.

Saati – Honorific for women, especially when addressing someone older.

shakti – An ethereal life-spark that comes from the Ayudena, to merge with the physical body of a destin as she is born from her pod. After a skakti becomes part of a living body, it is called "kana." When it leaves the body at the time of death, it becomes a shakti again and finds the Ayudena to be reabsorbed. Part of a mother's kana will transfer to her son at conception, to become his own kana/shakti.

shedding – As men pass middle age, their wrist scales will start to ooze a green fluid, in on-and-off cycles for about two years. It makes the scales burn, itch and ache. The only relief is to rinse in the waters of a destin lake, thus passing on DNA to future generations of destins.

sisters – When destins are born from the same lake on the same day, they are called sisters. They may or may not have the same dikshani (Amala).

Sixday Feast – Holiday at the end of the year with feasting, festivals, swimming tournaments, and waterball tournaments.

Skyfish – Another name for the Ayudena. The Ayudena is often depicted in art and sculpture as a golden fish in the sky. However, the real Ayudena has no eyes, fins, tail, etc. It has pale yellow scales on the surface, but its form is simply an elongated blob-like shape.

sliverbark – An experimental medicine used to suppress the immune system.

Swallowtail – Jayan's one-man canoe. It is small enough that he can carry it over his shoulder on portages.

tari oil – A common moisturizer used to prevent skin and scales from drying out. It is often offered to guests in the home.

tenday – Ten days = one week.

thirty and six – Slang for one year. A year is thirty tendays, plus one six-day "short week" at the end of the year, called the Sixday Feast.

Tines of Ayunath (the Tines) – Five immense sea stacks, located in the Southern Sea, just beyond the shore of Ayunath. One of them was destroyed by an earthquake five hundred years ago.

Waybender (aka *Hubli Waybender II*) – This canoe is lent by Master Dandalpan to Jayan, Charu, and Asta for their trip to Sindhupat.

wild destins – Primordial-like destins who are born in undiscovered shakti pools. If there is no Amala to perform diksha, the destin(s) will instinctively swim whatever waterway takes them to the ocean.

Made in the USA
Middletown, DE
05 March 2024

50212323R00136